The Last Box

First published in 2017 by Deerfold Press

www.singletobrighton.co.uk

Typesetting in Garamond by
Lilian Forshaw

All Illustrations © Lilian Forshaw
Printed in Great Britain by
Berforts South West Ltd, Hastings

Crime faction (fact and fiction)

A catalogue record of this book is available from
The British Library
ISBN 978-0-9954979-1-7

The Last Box
1765 – 1889

Lilian Forshaw

Author's notes
The Last Box forms a prequel to my trilogy of Granma Clara's life. She told it as passed down to her over the years by older family members. I thought it worth recording here as what my father called a "Crackin' good yarn."

Single to Brighton

All Change
1919-1940

Arrival
1941-1952

List of characters

Family around the fire Christmas evening 1951

Granma – Clara.

Dolly – Clara's daughter.

Artie – Dolly's husband.

Jimmie – Clara's son.

Hilda – Jimmie's wife.

Hetty – Artie's sister.

Arthur – Hetty's husband.

Lilian (Lily) – Dolly and Artie's daughter.

Characters in Amy's story.

Emily (nee Pilbeam) – Clara's mother.

John Pilbeam and his wife Annie(nee Hartshorn), Innkeepers at the Lamb Inn Hooe Pevensey Levels, East Sussex – Emily's parents.

Amy – Clara's great-great Grandmother born 1765.

Aunt Martha – Amy's life-long friend.

Jack Mortain and his wife Eleanor (nee Shoesmith) – Cloth Weavers. Amy's parents.

Cleone, Tibby and Tonia – Weavers. Amy's sisters.

Albert – Stone Mason Cleone's husband.

Sally – Amy's daughter from her first marriage.

Able Cakebread – Amy's first husband.

Helen and Elsa – Cakebread's twin sisters.

Paul Moreau – Helen's husband.

Tom Hartshorn – Carpenter. Amy's second husband.

James, Edwin and Joseph – Carpenters. Amy and Tom's sons.

George – Blacksmith. Tom's son from his first wife Molly.

Characters in Sally and Suzanne's story.

Suzanne Lavender – for whom Sally was nursemaid and friend.

Lord and Lady Lavender – Suzanne's parents.

Bebe – Lady Lavender's personal maid.

Carlotta Mcguire – Suzanne reborn.

Count Philippe d'Ville – Carlotta's husband.

Armand – the Count's Major Domo.

Rhoda, Dowager Countess d'Ville – Philippe's mother.

Vincent Moreau – Helen and Paul Moreau's son.

Maria Fitzherbert – Sally's friend and George VI mistress.

Zara, Ruben and Mario – Philippe's hounds.

Setting the Scene

December 25th 1951

"I may not see another Christmas." Granma Clara announced, as if this was a sudden thought. Then she added, "I've just remembered a story that I should tell you all." The room went quiet. It was late in the evening the family had been sitting around the fire in conversation long after a pleasant Christmas tea. Lifting the handle of the old copper coal bucket my Dad asked,

"Is it going to be a one bucket or two bucket story Clara?"

"Don't be so cheeky Artie." His sister Hetty said. Granma laughed,

"You won't change him Het. I'll try to keep it to a one bucket."

While Dad built up the fire, Uncle Arthur topped up the glasses and my Mum and Hilda, her sister in-law Jimmies wife, cut a few sandwiches.

"If Clara says it's something she should tell us I'd say it is gonna be two buckets worth!" whispered Hilda as they went out into the kitchen.

Meanwhile Granma Clara had been up to her bedroom and down beside her chair was an old oval shaped tin box, that was painted to look like wood.

Granma's story telling was legend in the family. Everybody sat back getting themselves comfortable in anticipation of, what my dad Artie, called a good yarn.

"I was 4 years old when I heard a hint of this story." Clara began, "It was when my mother took me to old granny Hartshorn's funeral tea. Mm, let me think now, that would have been in 1872. I had no idea what a funeral was, but I thought it must be a special tea party, because mum dressed herself all in black and tied a black bow in my hair." Clara paused to take a sip of her warmed ginger wine. "I can see that darkened room and hear the voices as if it were yesterday.

There was a little old lady sitting just inside the door she had a lacey cap on her head. Mum had to stoop down really low to kiss the lady's cheek.

'Clara, this is Aunt Martha.' Mum told me.

'Hallo child.' The lady said in a voice that sounded like a chirping bird.

I stood tucked in beside my Mother's knee watching lots of people coming into the room. Everybody appeared to rise around me; glum faced women sat down on straight backed chairs surrounded by layers of black stiff skirts. Men stood behind the ladies chairs holding their top hats sedately at shoulder level, leaving their uncovered bald heads shining white in the candle light; like mountain summits bobbing up against the ceiling. The only sound and colour in the room was the genteel plink of Granny's blue and white teacups and saucers. Somebody told my mother to lift me up above a long box, 'to take a last look at the dear departed,' I was surprised to see a face I recognised, although I couldn't understand why my Gan gan Amy was laying there so still." Granma paused, "I can just feel the times when I was cradled on her lap, she smelled sweetly of rosemary and somtimes of tangy mint. But most of all I remember her rocking with laughter in a way that made me happy. Oh, and I was sure the face in the big box smiled at me.

'Mummy, why ...?' Mum shushed away my question. A gruff voice from deep in a bonnet said,

'I heard she had a hard start.' Heads nodded in agreement. The lady topped with a little lace cap added firmly,

'Amy was a lovely girl.' That was quickly clipped by the gruff like woman, adding,

'But he was a beastly ma- -.' a sharp intake of breath through many sets of clenched teeth cut the speaker's flow. In the lull, a thud on the polished wood floorboards turned glances, lingering with distain, towards a large mothball; I had seen it fall from the folds of a skirt. Eyes followed as it rolled to a halt under the coffin. Then, I was certain Grandmother Amy Hartshorn really had smiled at me.

Silence again descended shrouding sad looks. A stomach rumbled.

'Sounds like you've left room for the beanfeast Lottie?' my Mother said under her breath, loud enough to be heard.

'Oh don't be so course Emily.' Her sister snapped.

A waft of cold air turned all heads. In the doorway stood a tall majestic old lady; her dress filling the space ablaze with marigold orange and pansy blue flowers; a grey fur edged short mauve coloured jacket shaped her body. Even more surprising was that she had one eye hidden by a shimmering silver patch. And, she was hatless. Shock vibrated through the company, the visitor's apparel was obviously so inappropriate to the occasion.

'That's the French woman.' Came a hiss, followed by,

'Hmph! a la mode I suppose?' a reply containing more than a hinted sneer.

With a cheeky wink from her visible eye and a nod to those that breathed, the lady walked unbidden across to the coffin followed by stern looks from the women and serupticious smiles from the men. The air seemed to prickle with expectation.

'Hallo Mother.' The visitor addressed Gran as if she was lying in her bed. For a long while the woman's faraway look filled time before she patted Gran's folded hands whispering, 'Thank you for Sally. Sleep well.' To my surprise my own Grandmother Annie, stood up and held out her hand,

'Carlotta?' she asked. The lady turned with such a graceful movement.

'Annie?' she replied. The two women went out of the room into the hallway where I saw them embrace then move away talking and out of my sight.

'Now that's how they used to treat funerals in my youth,' the lady with the lace cap said, 'gay colours and thanks for your company.'

'Aunt Martha how can you be so disrespectful.'

'Quite easily Lizzie, Amy would have laughed at all this heavy black sentimentality. We were close friends I know she had a happy fulfilled life.' Martha wasn't a blood relative but being Amy's life-long friend she was our Aunt of respect. Gruffy face hadn't given up and interrupting once again, blurting out,

'But what about the first one, they say he was a .... ?'

'A head turner, oh yes he was that alright, and more.' Martha announced,

'What more could there be? Tch! we all have our bad experiences.'

'It was more than a bad experience, Martha added, 'There's murder too.' In that instance a lady stood up saying briskly,

'Oh, come away George we're not listening to any more of this.' My mother's cousin by marriage, Amelia's imperious voice dropped to a whisper, 'Martha's always telling tall stories.'

'This is no tall story; perhaps now the time is right to reveal this episode of family history; I'm the last one left who can tell you.' Martha may have been 105 but her hearing was still sharp. Just as sharp came back the retort.

'Haw! But not murder, we don't have murders in our family.' proclaimed Amelia.

'That's what she thinks!' Martha shot back under her breath. 'What would the neighbours say.' My Mother mimicked behind her hand. Amelia gave Mother such a look, while tugging hard at her husband's coat sleeve.

'Amy was my Grandmother too you know, Melia.' George reminded his wife. Nevertheless he allowed her to drag him away; not before my mum caught his eye lifting a drinking motion to her lips as she mouthed, 'Come back later, new barrel.' George winked as his wife pushed him through the door in front of her, saying,

'A funeral is no place for this kind of talk, especially with the box still open.

'Oh close the box then.' Martha said with a brisk finality. 'My turn next.' And she laughed, a laugh tinged with sadness.

Then somebody noticed me. 'Hush the child in the room.' And I was swiftly hustled out and into the perfumed wake left by the beautiful woman with the eye patch."

"Hush the child," Clara repeated. "At the time I did not like being hustled out of the room, but I've never let a good story pass me by.

After the funeral Aunt Martha was staying with my Grandparents, John and Annie Pilbeam at their Inn, The Lamb on Pevensey Levels in East Sussex; and it was there she told the story of

Amy's life as only she could, because the pair had been close friends all their lives."

The story Clara always wanted to know

In the Christmas evening firelight a smile spread cheekily across Clara's face.

"I know what you all must be thinking. How could a four year old remember all that adult conversation?" That caused a collective release of breath accompanied by chuckles and grunts of assent. "Well I didn't of course. This is what I meant about hearing just a hint of a story at the funeral. I didn't hear Amy's whole story until years later. After great grandfather Johnny Pilbeam died in the summer of 1910 when I went over to the Lamb to help Mum and her sisters clear everything out before the Inn was sold."

Clara took a long pull at her now cooling ginger wine. "It was one of those odd coincidences that got us onto reminiscing about Granny Amy's funeral.

Mother and I thought we had finished the clearing so we were sitting having a cup of tea in the kitchen, when a voice from the attic above called out, 'Right ho, here we are folks, here's the last box.' followed by a hand descending from the loft holding and old tin bowler hat box."

"Yes this one down by my side." Clara told us, patting the top of the box before going on. "My mother was really surprised, saying,

'Oh, I know who that belonged to. It was Amy Hartshorn's. Aunt Martha had it at the funeral and later that evening --, Ah now wait a minute.' Mum lifted the box onto the table and started to ease open the heavy brass fastening. 'I wonder?' The tight lid finally opened with a sigh like puff. The smell of rosemary was unmistakable. I had to say, 'That's Amy's surely. And there I was a little child again, transported back in time, sitting on Amy's lap surrounded by that lovely rosemary perfume.

'You're right,' mum said, 'no mistaking that. And look, here, this is what I hoped I'd find, all the rolls of letters and a diary, Martha showed us that night. The night Martha told us the story dear old pompous Amelia didn't want to hear.'

And the story I wanted to know ever since I was hustled out of the room.

'It's a long story,' my Mother warned. Well you can imagine, I was eager to hear it all. And my mother, bless her, was keen to tell. Mum said, Martha told them something she would never forget.

'In every generation there is someone who passes on family stories, but I warn you, some of this tale I have to tell will be painful for you to hear, and for me to recall, but for the next generation, it IS something you need to know.'

Prequel: 1765 - 1889

PREQUEL: 1765 – 1889

1

Head Turner

"Oh yes, Abel Cakebread was a charmer, no mistaking that."
Martha recalled. "He could charm the socks of your cat!" My
father Bernie, who was the village butcher, said that everybody
who thought themselves anybody wanted to be associated with
Cakebread. The man so obviously had money but nobody knew
how he came by so much. All the locals knew his father had kept a
boat for fishing and a bit of smuggling down across the Channel in
the early 1770's.

After old man Cakebread died, word got back through the
grape vine that young Abel took a modest, but beautiful house some
distance from where the family grew up, – humph! He had more
than just the one. In another luxuriously furnished house, he kept
his two sisters, twins they were, dressing them in elegant expensive
clothes. Folks nearby sometimes caught sight of them when they
occasionally came and went from the house, the pair smiled but
never spoke and nobody ever met them socially. It was the local
women who Cakebread employed to look after his sisters who
whispered of the fashions and appointments in the house.

Cakebread was known to pay well and in gold. Although he
had got himself a second boat and kept it in constant use from the
harbour, two fishing boats wouldn't have brought in all that wealth.
The benefits gained by the few who knew his activities kept their
mouths shut tight; besides all those that he slipped a penny or two.
They thought him a good chap and although they called him 'Sir,'
he still seemed just like one of them.

Yes, he was seen around in Society, people thought they knew
him but no man could actually say they'd had a conversation with
him. Women openly made a play for him. His very aloofness drew
them on. He was so damnably good looking. He wore no wig,
although it was the fashion of the day, with his glossy raven hair
he didn't need one. Coupled with shapely eyebrows and long dark

lashes, to some, he was overwhelming – and blast the man, he could have worn anything – and he did. From fashionable town dashing, to fisherman's rough; with a body like his he cut a deuced fine figure. The women found him irresistible.

One lady was heard to comment, 'Have you felt his hands dear? He's no fisherman.' It made some men sick 'don't cher know. People either loved him or hated him there were no grey areas with Abel Cakebread.

"The very thought of him makes my blood curdle." Martha shuddered.

My father said the Town Council received substantial gifts of money, 'for their good deeds,' from this elegantly dressed man who stood so well, so well to be seen in his cut steel buckled shoes. Nobody local had ever received him at their table nor had they been at his, he didn't live in any town, and no town Mayor could, or would, say he knew Cakebread but his money was accepted no questions asked.

Ah! But who bought the neat elegant Merchant's house in the same cobble paved carriageway near to his sisters'. Somebody was in there preparing its readiness. Furnishings were delivered. Then it was locked up and left.

The two boats the 'Lucky Maid' and the 'Abel" went out regularly, making good hauls of fish and lobsters, the catches sold and his men were well paid. When his shoreline sales were completed, Cakebread mounted his horse that was always at the ready in a hostelry by the harbour, and rode away to nobody knew where.

It seemed he was accepted for his very presence; he was an enigma, even a chameleon.

2

Unforgiven Moments

Martha said Amy was a bit over a year older than her, being born in 1765 the youngest of four daughters to Jack Mortain, a Weaver and his wife Eleanor, who was a Shoesmith. The family lived on the ground floor of a long sturdy timber framed cottage, the floor above was one open space fronted by a north facing stretch of shuttered windows, being their workshop where four wood framed looms stood. The building was already a hundred years old when Jack, on his marriage to Eleanor, inherited it from his father. Two generations back Jack's Grandfather and his twin brother had built their loom floor; supported by three heavy beams, high above the living area to gain every hour of light available in the day for weaving, and chose the valley of the river Rother, on the borderland of Kent and Sussex, where the water ran in abundance to wash their fleeces ready for spinning and weaving.

Amy's two elder sisters were earthenware plain and mousey haired, Tibby and Tonia, steadfast workers at their looms; they became finger fast, throwing the shuttles like sparkling shards back and forth across the warp. Ah, when we youngsters were allowed to stand at the top of the ladder on the weaving floor, it was a thrilling sight, to watch those two girls work. Amy's regular job was to gather flowers; wild garlic and walnuts in season to dye their parent's wool. Amy, described by a family member as having, porcelain pink skin and golden hair, had a nak of finding and preparing ingredients along the field hedgerows that made the most unusually attractive coloured dyes. 'Sun blessed bright our Amy,' Aunt Martha chuckled, saying, "While she was little and rounded I was tall with long hair. Yes I was. The last of my family; 'a surprise present' Ma used to call me. Pa laughed, he said I was skinny. Well, that didn't stop Amy and me being bosom pals."

Times came, as Amy emerged from childhood, when gleaning among the hedgerow foliage she often felt the whine of a tiny stone passing close to her ear, she did not flinch.

"Take no notice, keep going." Tibby had warned. Amy well knew it was Jeb Watt who was trying to catch her attention with his catapult, while on the job for farmer Garth. Across the other side of the field the air would suddenly be ripped by a clacking wooden bird scarer; Jim Watt sent up the crows for his brother's sure aim. Few crows escaped Jeb's catapult and Amy had not escaped Jeb's eye.

The Mortain family was well known at markets for their durable warm cloth; richly coloured deep damson purple; mossy yellows and spring green made into good substantial shawls and especially the enveloping riding cloaks fashioned by their Mother Eleanor. Tough wearing coveralls that kept the rain out were sought after at village markets in east Sussex and west Kent. Just like the characters of the family themselves, tough hard working, used to long hours regular and dependable.

On quarter days the whole family left their work to visit one of the markets. Setting out well before dawn the cart piled high with their carefully folded products protected from any rain with a fine cover woven from grass by Eleanor in the early years of her marriage. Father sat up on the cart driving while his wife and daughters walked beside and behind, giving their old horse an extra hand up the hills.

If you didn't get to Rye or Appledore very early in the morning and on a special once a year occasion over to Canterbury, you wouldn't get their garments unless you had given an order to be made. Dealers came from London to buy almost anything the family made, although there were never many items spare.

When selling was finished their Father would allow his wife and daughters to wander the stalls for 'their little fripperies', as he called them; whilst he indulged himself in a pot of ale as he did business with the sheep farmers for their wool. Eleanor, she was a sweet lady, bought the household basic provisions. Then with the women all sat on the back of the cart their horse pulled the family back home.

There was an elder sister but she had decided early in her life that weaving wasn't for her. Cleone Mortain went for a sewing maid to Lord and Lady Lavender's at their great house, surrounded by a moat, toward Canterbury way. The Lavender family already had five children in the nursery so all three nursemaids, two nursery maids and a wet nurse, were kept busy. Cleone could catch a coach to bring her down across the Romney Marsh and into Sussex and home once a year and she was content with that. Being in service gave her more freedom and friends than under her father's roof. Much as she loved them all she was happy to leave again after her few days stay.

"I know young Amy was the one Cleone missed most." Martha declared.

It was 15 year old Amy who caught somebody else's eye. Of all the local wenches he picked her. The rider saw her at market one day when he stopped at the Smith to have his horse re-shod. Amy, petite with well rounded hips held his attention.

Mr Mortain crowed on and on about how he had sold a particular riding cloak to a very wealthy looking man who placed an order last month; what was more, the same man came to the next market meeting ordering two more cloaks, this time requesting a lighter weave for Ladies carriage wear. Jack Mortain was really proud of these two cloaks the colours his wife and daughters achieved with the glut of elderberries were especially attractive this time. The man even gave an order for a third Lady's cloak and then stood talking to Mr Mortain.

Jack thought him to be a very important man. He was tall, very well dressed with longish glossy black wavy hair tied back in a modest but stylish bow. Yes, his clothes were expensive and he wore a clean wholesome silk neckerchief. Why would this rider want his family's rustic cloaks? Jack asked himself. Well, of course it was because his cloaks were weather proof. That's why. The Mortain's cloaks kept the man's elegant riding coat and breeches, down to his highly polished boots well covered. Jack knew all the answers.

The family's sales did well, but never quite well enough to replace their elderly cart. And honestly they should have put poor Betsie out to pasture, she could only just manage to pull their stock to market once a quarter whilst the women walked. Young Amy walked both ways and often stayed with the horse at market to make sure she was fed and groomed and sometimes given a look over by the Farrier. Amy noticed the man watching her from where he stood across the square. Somehow she could not but notice, for his gaze did not leave her even when people spoke to him and he gave his replies joining the laughter and joking – they liked him. She noticed how by sleight of hand coins were passed on then a bright smile would flash across an Osler's face or the Smithy's boy pull his forelock nodding his thanks. The Smith doffed his greasy old cap to this man and got on with shoeing his great black horse, while another owner finding himself with a second ale in front of him just waited a little longer to have his horse attended to without even showing annoyance.

Betsie nearly didn't have a cart to pull one day. Jack was forced to spend some money for Will Hartshorn to do repairs.

"Lookee 'ere Jack," pointed out the Carpenter, "you can't go on repairin' wood that's rotten. This has got to be the last time. Why don't you get yerself a new wagon man – ye could do with somethin' bigger – those women o' yorn work hard enough for their bread!"

"That's no business of yours Will Harshorn, I'll take my business elsewhere if you won't suit me." Jack Mortain shouted his irritation.

"Now come on Jack, don't get the rats – I'm only tryin' to 'elp yer 'afore that old cart really lets yer down."

It being shearing time Jack took advantage that market day to collect their bales of fleeces as well as having Betsie looked at by the Farrier who said he'd clean her teeth too – 'poor ol' creecher'.

That's when it happened. Jack Mortain left his old cart nearby the wool merchant's barn ready for loading and some silly devil miss-hooked a wool bale onto the hoist so that the bale fell heavily on to Jack's cart. Smashed it to match wood didn't it. Well, the onlookers said that it wasn't much more than the ol' cart was worth anyways besides being lucky that the poor ole nag wasn't in the shafts at the time.

When Jack went round to Wills' carpenter's shop he was told good 'n' well that nobody could build him a cart in an afternoon. Jack nearly exploded. Well he did explode, at Will for being so direct, but it weren't Carpenter's fault, after all he had been telling him months back he needed a new wagon.

"Mr Mortain can have mine Mr Hartshorn, I won't need it today." Jack was taken aback – nobody had ever helped him out before.

"You can borrow it man. Your need is more than mine today."

"Go on Jack – you won't get a better offer on Market day." Will advised.

Jack was usually a belligerent man but, just in time, decided his old tune was the wrong one to play, and so an unusual smile came onto his face – he thanked the man – just like Amy had noticed others did. The owner of the wagon was the rider who had purchased four cloaks a month or so back.

"Thankee Sir, you're very generous."

"No thanks needed. Get your bales loaded for home."

When the Farrier brought Betsie round to the back of Will Hartshorn's carpenter's shop and saw the new heavy wagon he stopped in his tracks. Betsie, whose bridle he was holding stopped too, but not for the same reason. Farrier Chapman stopped and stared at the wagon he'd been told to hitch Betsie into, then he laughed out loud. Coming round from behind the wagon where he'd been making a space among the fleeces for his daughter's to sit on their journey home Jack barked,

"Wot yer laughin' at?"

"Well, heh, heh, this poor nag could just about manage that old cart of yorn but don't expect her to get this wagon more than a couple of steps. It'd kill 'er!"

Jack actually looked contrite.

"Drat!" he half swallowed under his breath. Much to his wrath – partly with himself, for having to put his hand into his best going to market trousers pocket to hire a good strong horse to get the heavily loaded wagon back home; although not before he had slipped round to the abattoir and got a shilling back in his pocket for Betsie.

It was the first time the women had experienced a comfortable ride. This wagon was expertly sprung. Poor Amy was tearful for her beloved Betsie.

3

The Price

Over the following two months Jack asked around at the hostelries, the Smithy and the various Merchants and of course Will Hartshorn. None of them had seen the man since he'd loaned Jack his wagon. When Jack went to pay for the extended hire of the horse he was told the hire charge had been paid for the next three months. Jack Mortain couldn't make head or tail of it. Nobody could be that stupid with their money, so he just forgot the man. He needed the horse.

"Where's that girl gorn again? Tibby, 'ave you sin your young sister?"

Tibby called out to Tonia "Where's Amy?"

"She's out collectin' 'erbs.'" replied Eleanor.

"Damn silly 'erbs. What's the matter with the girl?"

"She's doin' what she knows about, Father."

"There's no time for doin' wot yer want 'ere, I can't do wot I want".

"No neither can we." Tib replied under her breath.

"Whisht girl," cautioned her mother, "you'll get us all whipped."

"Oh no, Mother, no more of that lark" retorted Tonia "I've told 'im I'm off if 'e touches us again."

"Don't talk silly me gal. Where would you go?"

"Never you mind Ma, wot yer don't know yer can't tell."

Coming through the back yard Amy overheard that exchange and carried on busying herself laying out the herbs to dry. Only fifteen but Amy had already made up and sold her mixtures and salves for women's needs when the family took their wares to the market. Granma Shoesmith – her mother Eleanor's mother - had been teaching Amy about the flora ever since the little girl could toddle the lanes and byeways around her Gran's cottage on the Romney Marsh. Amy often accompanied her Gran to her local village market, selling the salves she had helped to make. That was when Amy was too young for Jack Mortain to use the child to help his wife with no more than teasing out the fleece for her spinning. There was something else her Grandmother had encouraged Amy to do, that was to learn to read. In the church they sat side by side whilst her Grandmother said the Ten Commandments from memory for Amy to follow each word that was painted, gold against black on the Decalogue boards above the pew. Then one day a lady who purchased salves from Grandma Shoesmith gave Amy a small box containing five Chap books (stories for children); saying she noticed how the little girl had been standing looking intently and mouthing the words on a poster pasted to the wall by the Cattle market.

"These will help you to learn." she bent low whispering in the child's ear, "but don't let your father know you can read my dear."

Her father called the days his youngest daughter spent in her Grandmother's company, 'a waste of time' and threatened to tie the child to the loom. That is, when he could catch her. Some herbs needed picking when the dew was upon them so Amy would often skip off out before her father rose from his bed even though he himself had to be an early riser.

One day he did tie her ankle to the heavy wood frame of the loom she was working at. It was the only time. She worked all that day in silence, as usual, even on into the night by candle light until her head dropped onto the cloth. Her mother untied the child and put her to bed.

"Keep out'a this woman. I WILL have my family do as I say."

Next morning Amy was gone. They didn't see her for two days. Unable to find her at her Grandmother's cottage, Jack ranted until he caught sight of her again in the back yard where she was laying out her gathered herbs. Hitting the base of the drying tray with the flat of his hand he sent the contents and split wood flying in all directions. His arm rose again at Amy this time, but as it descended onto the little girl's head another hand broke its passage. The face close to his spoke all he needed to know. His angry, "Get back to that loom girl," issued from deep in his throat out of barely suppressed anger. The four women sat down at the looms and fell to work with a will that surprised John Mortain. All that day he could feel the undercurrent and that fuelled his ire even more. The women stopped to take a bite middle day working on to dusk then laid down their shuttles before a candle needed lighting. From that day on they set their own daily pattern.

"Bloody, bloody women." he wailed.

When she came home on her next annual visit Cleone brought an old unused copy book from the Lavender children's nursery. Amy was a very bright child and quick to learn. Cleone, who had secretly taught herself to write from this book, taught her young sister to write her name and copy down the Ten Commandments from the Decalogue. Before she returned to Moat Mount Cleone showed the little girl how to fold a piece of paper and seal it, just as she had herself observed, telling Amy that if she ever wanted help she could write a note heading it, 'For Cleone,' and addressing it to the Housekeeper, saying some of the other staff received letters that way; Cleone said she would send her replies to Will Harsthorn's Carpenter shop for his wife Liz to take them in, Amy could ask if there was a letter when she visited on Market days.

"But don't forget sweetheart, let Will read it to you." Cleone had reminded her.

Some days after that family contretemps who should stop outside the yard but the handsome man on a huge powerful black horse. He did not dismount. Jack went out to greet him.

"How's business Mr Mortain?"

"No so bad Sir. I must thank you for your wagon. Perhaps you will tell me how much I owe you for its use. Oh an' the horse too, I'm told."

Abel Cakebread dismounted and hung his horse's reins over the rail. He slowly withdrew each leather glove and folded them together holding the pair down beside his thigh. An elegant well breached thigh, worth looking at. Taking off his large soft brimmed rabbit fur riding hat, he ran his fingers through the neatly trimmed black hair lifting the waves to fall full and frame his face. Jack Mortain found himself watching all this preening surprised at his own patience.

"Mr Mortain. You asked me a direct question. I am a direct man, payment for the wagon and horse; your youngest daughter."

Jack was at first rather bewildered. Cakebread smiled and l aid his hand on Jack's shoulder turning him away from the cottage and walked him a few steps into the lane, onto neutral ground.

"Well," Jack sucked in air through his teeth slowly to retrieve his thoughts and understand what it would mean to his weaving business. "Well now, it would mean I would be losing a skilled pair of hands." Yes, he thought privately, but too often away from the loom. Cakebread said nothing. "An' she's a very good dyer, makes our very best colours."

Cakebread made no reply,

The two men stood shoulder to shoulder looking across the Marsh to the sea and the town far away on a hilltop. Jack couldn't move, the hand on his shoulder stilled him. It had that effect. He turned his head towards sight of another low hill. Far to his left one of the churches where's said Smugglers rested their goods. Everything related and unrelated seemed to go through his mind – all his life afore him somehow. It came back to him then, that he wasn't very good at this negotiating and bartering business. He'd never had any luck amongst the smuggling families. They always got the better of him, he was fortunate to have extricated himself when he did, it was the only situation he'd unwittingly achieved by having a cart too small to carry contraband goods, otherwise he would have been inveigled into stowing stuff under his wool. Yes, he thought, this wagon and horse had come his way just at a necessary time - or -would it bring an unwanted cost? Amy was beginning to cost him. Had he known this daughter of his could read, he might have rated her value a tad higher.

For once Abel Cakebread misread a man and succumbed to another's silence.

"Would this be of any use to you?" The words were almost inaudible as the gold coins slid smoothly into the father's hand, but had he known this girl could read the sum he handed out might have been somewhat lower. Consequently Jack's eyes lit up, but he tried not to show it.

"You'd marry her wouldn't you? Make it proper for my family?"

"My God man whatever do you take me for? Of course that's what I want, a wife. No less." Oh yes, Abel Cakebread was a charming man.

PREQUEL: 1765 – 1889

4

The Deal

No, he couldn't take her now. That would be unseemly, Jack Mortain was adamant with outsiders when he had to be. Yes the deal was done but he was determined to see his daughter properly wed. It would look bad for him if she wasn't.

"When is the girl's time of the month Mr Mortain?" Cakebread was getting too personal now, but Jack accepted the man had his rights. He wanted his purchase delivered at the opportune time. Jack replied,

"You will have to ask her mother for that information. Eleanor." he called, causing his wife to leave her work and walk out across the yard to where the two men stood in the lane; he then deliberately turned away.

"Has your youngest daughter seen her menses yet Mrs Mortain?" Cakebread smiled but was quite brisk expecting no more than a yes or no. Eleanor was startled at such a choice of subject. She could only but be truthful, "Yes sir, she has."

"Good. And when is her time of the month Mrs Mortain?"

"Tis now sir." she found herself imparting before she had time for thought.

"Thank you." Turning to Jack Mortain, Cakebread swung his hat back on his head and smartly pulled on his gloves.

"Then it shall be in two weeks time. Make your arrangements as you will."

Cakebread put out his hand to Eleanor. She was still rooted to the spot in surprise, let alone horror; for this was the first she had heard of the deal. He had to physically take her hand because she was unable to respond. Gently he pressed a sovereign into her palm. Closing the limp fingers round the coin he quietly said,

"Buy your daughter some pretty petticoats Mrs Mortain. Good day to you both." He was up in the saddle and on his way before either could reply. "Two weeks." he called back over his shoulder, touching the brim of his hat in salute.

So that was it. Jack Mortain had been suspicious of the ease that a wagon and horse had come his way and to the payment; well, beggars can't be choosers. As Eleanor walked slowly back into the yard her husband had his back to her, urinating into the deep piss pot that stood just inside the yard gate. He knew she wouldn't approach and speak to him when he was replenishing the Mordant liquor; that was men's work; he had always made that clear to the women. They might be clever with finding the ingredients to make the dyes but none of that was any use without the men's urine to fix the colour. Jack was always ostentatious in his replenishing at the pot as if to say, I'm the master here. He encouraged the local men to give freely of their abundance. Not all were inclined that way though.

* * * *

"Jeb was heartbroken when he heard Amy's future had been settled for her." Martha said, "He was a strong likeable lad. He left the village and went for a soldier. The family never heard from him again; I know, for he was my brother Jeb."

5

Ordeal

Martha paused, took a sip from her gill of ale after telling us there had been a few words mumbled over a prayer book in the church. Then wiping her lips with the back of her hand she sighed deeply and went on.

"Years later Amy told me there was nobody there to greet them at his grey stone house. He hadn't spoken a word in the hour since he had helped her up to sit sideways across in front of him on his great horse."

* * * *

Dusk was gathering as they arrived in the stable yard, he dismounted, linked the horse's rein into a metal ring on the wall by a door, swung his saddle bags across his shoulder, lifted Amy down, rapped on the stable groom's door with his riding crop as he passed, walking her to the house. Inside candles lit a small hallway; she had not known what to expect, the atmosphere struck warm and mellow.

"You must be tired after our journey, wife?" he didn't wait for her answer, just took up a candlestick and motioned her to go up the wide polished oak stairs in front of him. The air became warmer as they went up to the floor above. Three doors on the landing were closed, one other slightly ajar, he indicated her through. His candle illuminated a glow of rich colours blending tapestry hangings and little oval miniature pictures. A fire in the grate gently crackled throwing its light onto the two low padded chairs either side of an elegant round galleried table holding two heavy glasses and a tall silver collared decanter jug. When Abel took a taper and lighted the candles in the small silver double wall sconces, Amy could see a lavishly soft piled four poster bed dominated the room. Slumping down in one of the chairs he ordered her,

"Here pull these damn boots off me." Amy was used to that tone of order from her father. "Now you can change – there, behind the screen." he pointed as he untied his stock. Amy had never changed her clothes with a man in the same room before, not even her father.

"Hhaw!" there was somebody in there with her. The shock made her topple back against the screen.

"What's the matter woman?" he must have heard her surprised breath intake, "Get on with it." Amy had never before seen her reflection so vividly clear. This was the first mirror to see her, and in full length. She felt uncomfortable all over again, having another figure watching her so closely.

Across the curving back of a day bed lay a satin night shift and dressing coat in deep ruby plum; a choice of colour much too old to flatter the pale skin of such a young girl. The silk fabric was so soft and light against her skin. When she came from behind the screen, the dressing coat tied tightly round her, he was pouring a little hot water from a small copper kettle, over two sugar lumps in a glass of golden liquid.

"Sit here and take this drink. It will make you sleep well tonight. Go on. Go on, try it."

"I've never had strong drink before."

"That's alright you're a married woman now." He lolled back in the chair opposite her. He was sweating and seemed short of breath.

The fire felt much hotter as she sipped the sweet drink. From a few feet away his eyes bored into her.

"Stand up. Take that dressing coat off." She was so hot she did so and made to sit again.

"Stay standing," he ordered, "now take that nightgown off." She didn't

"Go on." he urged. But she'd be naked. So she didn't do it.

"Go on," he was irritated now, "I want to see what I've got."

A sudden rush of inhaled breath lunged at her and she was flung onto the bed.

He must have been expert in taking off nightgowns because she didn't know where it went. Arms and legs wide he was on her and in her causing her dreadful pain taking all the breath from her body while he let out shocking loud horrible animal roaring's. Heaving to free her arms she laid the flats of her hands against his abdomen.

"You don't need to touch me. Take your hands off me woman," She didn't.

"I do not want you touching me." His voice lowered to a menacing angry pitch.

Damn you, she thought. Elbows and knees would do for her but her efforts were nothing against his superior strength.

"Don't fight me," he ordered. "I won't have you fighting me." His full body weight stopped her movement, almost stopped her breathing. No use struggling.

Suddenly he rolled over fast asleep. It hadn't lasted many minutes but her whole body wanted to cry, to scream and cry. Nobody told her this is what men did to women. Had her mother had to endure this kind of assault, because that's what she felt it was; an assault.

Trying to move without disturbing him she realised then how horribly sore she felt and nearly screamed out loud when she saw the blood on the covers. Stealthily she pulled herself across the bed. A great hand clamped itself around her ankle. The heavy ring he wore on his right thumb gouging through her skin to the bone.

"You will stay put." Before she could take a breath he was on her again hands everywhere. No part of her body was private. She had no breath to fight for the pain just got worse.

When he'd finished he said, "Now raise your bottom up," he pushed a pillow under her lower back, "pull your knees up, go on bend your legs. Put the flat of your feet on the bed. Now stay like that until I say you can move." Throwing a cover over her body up to her chin he left the room taking the candles with him. Just the small candle sconces on the wall remained giving a glimmer of light, although by then nearly burned out.

Frightened at what he might do next, she remained in that position for the rest of the night.

The experience left young Amy's body shaking involuntarily, not in terror, but in deep emotional shock over which she had no control. The spasm lasted until broken by the release of tears. All she wanted was her mother. How could her father have given her away to this ... oh no the very thought of the man created in her a shivering effect of recoiling horror. She had to destroy any thought of him from her mind. Finally she slept through sheer exhaustion.

6

Controlled

When Amy woke the room was dark except for a sliver of light between the curtains, making her think it may be the middle of the day, but she couldn't really tell. The bedclothes were stuck to her legs with congealed blood. Oh, the pain and soreness returning with every movement. Taking a deep breath she wrapped a shawl around herself, taking tiny steps she crossed the room to pull back the heavy curtains. She did not recognise the view she saw out across the countryside; a long view without a break; no trees, no hills, a few sheep dotted far and near under a sky bigger than the land. The high angle of the light told her it was later than noonday and she was desperate to pass water. Eleanor had taught her daughters to keep themselves clean, but where would she find the deep earthenware lidded pot with its glazed innards like her mother kept. From her earliest memory Amy had taken her turn each morning to empty their night soil into the village midden. Looking back into the room she saw the fire had been built up and a can of warm water stood beside a wash bowl; towels hung on a wooden rail and there under the bed was a gleaming white china pot with flowers painted all around. Cleone had told her how the Lavenders had beautifully decorated piss pots, they called them Chamber pots and this must be one of them. She would worry about where it was emptied later for now it was her saviour.

Standing on one of the towels Amy cleaned her body down and bathed her ankle. Somebody had left a new under chemise, petticoats and a light linen dress folded over a nearby chair. Every movement an agony, making her thoughts go to the women who bought her Grandmother's salves. At the time she had no idea those women's troubles had anything to do with what men did, nobody had told her anything about men. Finding her valise beside the dressing chest, she was relieved to find a pot of her Grandmother's salve tucked well down to the side. Now she knew from personal experience, the soothing effect that its application would, 'cleanse and heal,' as she'd heard her Grandmother tell the women who made their purchases from her in the market. At just fifteen she had only recently learned about her menses, but being the youngest child did not really know what they were for.

Crossing the room she noticed there was another mirror over the dressing chest and small mirrors backing the candle sconces; already refreshed with new candles, so many mirrors in one room when she had never before seen a single glass mirror.

Opening the bedroom door gently, just in case he was nearby, Amy edged painfully down the stairs she had come up just a few hours ago. The house was cool and quiet.

Peering through a part open door she saw a well appointed sitting parlour, with floor to ceiling windows, along one wall, covered in fluid white lace curtains allowing light to flood the room. Each side of the widow pale coloured drapes trailed in neatly placed pools on the floor, that was covered in layers of rugs, patterned in an arrangement of swirls, stripes and blocks making her gasp in awe at the variety of rich colours and designs. Sofly upholstered elegant chairs and a chaise lounge set around with small tables; there were wine glasses and decanters, pictures on the walls, all things outside her knowledge.

Tearing her gaze away she followed the passageway that went alongside the stairs; she had expected to find a scullery, but instead there was quite a spacious kitchen. A large table stood in the centre of a flag stoned floor, to her right an oven set in a chimney area beside a bright fire and kettles waiting for use. To her left a stone sink with a pump handle, with a window behind. In a straight back chair beside a door sat a small figure, it moved, Amy jumped violently finding she had been watched in silence by another human in such close proximity, this following her recent experience made her reaction all the more sharp.

"Oh, you startled me," Amy held her hand against her thumping heart, "I didn't know there was anybody else in the house."

Getting up from the straight backed chair, stood a girl no older than herself; white cap, white apron, brown woollen dress, hands clasped together in front of her waist, head bowed gave a bobbed curtsey; then waited for her orders.

"Do you live here?" It was such a relief to find somebody other than him.

"No madam. I come in from the village every day. My name's Tilly."

"Was it you who left the warm water for me?"

"Yes please 'm."

"Thank you so much Tilly." The girl blushed deeply.

"Tilly can you get me something to eat, I'm famished?"

"Yes, I will bring it to you in the breakfast room Madam." A room just for breakfast Amy looked this way and that.

"The breakfast room is through here Madam."

"No, I'll sit here at the table Tilly."

"Oh no Madam, please use the breakfast room." The girl almost pleaded.

Amy went into the breakfast room, as she had been requested and in no time at all she was served hot chocolate to drink. Never had she tasted such a drink, it filled her mouth and her senses, her whole body. A piece of bread some butter and a pot of wonderful honey was enough to bring life back into her wracked body.

So overtaken by this new sensation, she did not at first notice the breakfast room window gave onto a view opposite to the one she had looked out on from the bedroom above and oh joy, way across the horizon she could see the familiar hill with its town on the top rising like a cottage loaf out of the flat land, and not far beyond a shining line of the sea. Piece of bread in her hand she stood looking and munching, her fear subsiding a little.

Now she knew where she was in the landscape. Now she didn't feel so alone.

Picking up her plate, cup saucer, spoon and knife she went with them through to the kitchen. Tilly jumped up.

"Oh please Madam, please you don't have to do that madam, Master says I have to wait on you. Please, there's a bell on the table." Amy whispered a, "Sorry," realising Cakebread's heavy hand controlled everything he owned.

Back up in the bedroom, after her meal, she found the bed had been freshly made, clean washing water and towels and the fire made up. How did Tilly manage it in that short time? Amy had never been a maid servant, never set foot in anywhere more than a working familys' cottage. She had no experience of the practices in a house belonging to the wealthy.

"Master says to make sure you put your feet up Madam." Tilly was there in the room behind her motioning to a chair, tucking cushions round and pushing a footstool under her feet; a glass of water stood on a table by her elbow. "What would you like for luncheon Madam?" Amy hadn't thought that far ahead. A shawl was layed across her knees. My goodness she felt overwhelmed, I'm fifteen not fifty Tilly can't be more than my own age. "The Master left me a hen to roast for you. Will that suit?"

"Yes thank you that will be lovely. Thank you Tilly." Amy just wanted to be left alone, alone to think. Could she go back to her parent's home? At least she felt she now knew the direction to take. But, he says she belongs to him and when she tried the house door on her way through the downstairs hall it was locked and no key in evidence. How could she run? Anyway for the moment she could not move without causing herself more pain. For now, she was a prisoner.

When, some days later, Cakebread entered into her solitary life again, the first thing he asked was, had she been sick?

"No sir, I'm quite well, thank you."

"How do you like your new home Madam?"

That night he came to her bed again. He didn't seem quite so bestial. More deliberate, insistent, nevertheless the pain she was forced to endure was, if anything, was more excruciating than the first time. Before he departed the next morning, a small tapestry frame was set up in the bedroom with a needlework box full of neat hanks of coloured yarns. It made her happy but did nothing to quell the horror the pain and her desperate need for her Mother. She felt sure her Mother and sisters had no idea where she was.

As she healed inside, it was her damaged ankle causing her to limp, that made her feel like an old woman. Pain aside, it would not prevent her venture around the house to look further, this time inside the rooms, where everything seemed so perfect, so untouched, as if it wasn't there to be used. Amy saw it all as fascinating. Finding her-self marvelling at a beautiful soft leather folder; when on lifting the corner, saw it covered a few sheets of writing paper; nearby lay a stick of sealing wax. Cleone had told her about the wax to seal letter folds. She had never seen all the paraphernalia of writing before, apart from the small feather with the cut tip Cleone gave her when she practiced writing. There it all was on Cakebread's desk in the sitting room. Pulling out a shallow drawer, just for a peep, she saw two long white feathers one cut ready to use the other as nature made it, the only item she couldn't see was ink. Ah, but she knew how to make dyes so ink shouldn't be beyond her. As she lifted the first sheet of writing paper she stopped pushed the drawer closed. No, something brought her up short, reminding her of her own father's determination; it was as strong as this deviousness. Telling her-self she should never forget this, she left the room deciding to take time to think things over more carefully.

When looking curiously through her close surroundings in the bedroom, she noticed one of the lower drawers in the linen press had two precious leaves of paper beneath the linen sheets. Withdrawing the lower piece she could make a fold giving her enough for four letters and as far as a writing implement was concerned, well she certainly could not touch the great quills she had seen in the drawer but she could search under the trees in the garden for a Magpie feather and whittle a fine tip on one of those. Amy determined nothing would stop her. The home made quill well suited the style of lettering she had learned from the church engraving that had been her tutor.

On one sheet Amy wrote to her sisters addressing it to Liz Hartshorn; telling where she thought she was and a little of what had happened in the weeks since she left home. She knew she couldn't write any details of the ugly happenings because Will Hartshorn would read the note to her mother and sisters and of course she wouldn't embarrass him or upset her mother, she knew this marriage wasn't their doing, Eleanor would have had no say in the matter. In her first letter, addressed to Liz Hartshorn, Amy referred to her mother as 'Shoe,' so when Will Hartshorn read the letter aloud they knew who it was meant for and would put it aside for Eleanor when she and the girls called in to see Liz on the next market day.

The second letter she sent to the housekeeper at Moat Mount near Canterbury for her sister Cleone. Amy didn't know if Cleone had been told what had happened to her, so in tiny writing she told Cleone as much as she was able to get on one side of paper. Folded and addressed, the letters needed sealing. She couldn't possibly use the new stick of sealing wax. Amy remembered she had seen the wax in the kitchen drawer, ready to use for sealing the tops of preserving jars. That would have to suffice. Amy asked her sisters not to reply until she found a safe way of receiving letters. The other two pieces of paper she kept tucked safely away for later use.

Over the weeks Tilly had become a little more talkative. After all they were the same age and background. Amy could only hope she could trust her.

Maybe Tilly would take the two letters to the Post coach for Canterbury? She had to trust somebody. Surely the whole world couldn't have turned against her?

Cakebread's reappearances were as sudden as his disappearances. There was no conversation beyond what he wanted to know or orders he threw at her. One question was always the same,

"Are you being sick in the mornings?" and

"How do you like your new home?" And now,

"Are you pleased with your serving girl?"

"Very well Sir, thank you."

"Then I will see you later my dear." Her heart sank. Did that mean what she thought it meant?

Late that night when she was then well asleep she was woken by this rough man. Bedclothes thrown back he thrust his part clothed body onto hers with even more vigour than the first time. Again he left but this time not for very long, he was persistant until one morning a month later she was sick and he was there to witness her discomfort. From that moment on he was all consideration. Nothing spared. Tasty titbits that he told her his sisters had sent; there were fruit jellies and savoury sambals. He never touched Amy again in that way. He still came and went with many days of absence between his reappearances. He left small bags of money on the dresser for her needs. What needs? She tucked them away.

"Get the air my dear. Sit out in the sun. Do your tapestry. Collect your herbs in the fields. Take your maid with you." But he would not hear of her walking to market selling her herbals. Not now, it wasn't seemly for a married woman to walk, definitely not. After all she had no need for money. He set up a loom and provided spinning items, teasels and fleeces. She was to consider herself a lady of leisure, a mother to be.

Tilly was her only companion; Amy decided to teach the girl to read so that she could check the village post drop at the cross roads. Cakebread must never know his wife received any communication from home and even less that she could read and write or that Tilly could read. Later, in secret moments, she taught the young maid to write her own name, like Amy had been, she was quick to learn. Tilly's mother only heard from her daughter that she had met girls of her own age at market and they were all learning to write their own names and practice on each other. Amy told Tilly to tell her Mother, "It's a game we play." Nevertheless, confined and alone with her own thoughts, Amy knew she dare not trust anybody in the village.

PREQUEL: 1765 – 1889

7

Locked away

Tilly overjoyed at finding herself a friend and confidant became a mine of information. Amy learned more about her two sisters in law. She had known of their existence but she hadn't realised they lived so few paces away. At first she was surprised they had not visited her, until Tilly told her the women were rarely seen – but then nor after all was she ever seen outside the walled garden. They were all three kept locked away.

Tilly said the sister's maid had told her the two women slept most of the daytime especially after good clear nights out at sea. That puzzled Amy. She heard they bathed and oiled their bodies a lot and a woman went in to do their hair. Dressmakers delivered dresses, laces and shawls and their brother bought them fur capes.

If they ventured out to sit in the garden umbrellas graced their shoulders or awnings were spread from house to tree and back creating wider shades over all to keep their skin soft and white.

Cakebread had not encouraged her to make any contact. Amy resolved to change that although she had no idea how they would receive her. On a day when he came from his dressing room arrayed in fine linens; coat, breeches and highly polished riding boots, finally taking up an elegant hat, she knew he would be going further afield and away for longer than on the days he dressed like a fisherman.

As soon as the coast was clear she sent Tilly to enquire if the two sisters would receive her. The maid knew the safe pathway connecting the houses out of sight from the village gaze. Just minutes after receiving their invitation Amy was in a heavily draped and cushioned sitting room surrounded by the cloying scent of flowery perfumes, an atmosphere with which she found it hard to cope in her pregnant state.

Helen, the younger twin put her arms around Amy kissing her on both cheeks; standing back to look into Amy's face she said,

'Amy, you are so welcome, we are pleased you've finally found the courage to come to us.' They knew her name? Oh yes they knew all about her, what were trusted serving maids for after all. That broke the ice they laughed for sheer relief.

Their friendship was immediate and grew the more with comfort in mutual condition. Apart from their names, Helen and Elsa, she knew little about them. The two women were reticent about their own recent experiences so it was some time before Amy heard anything of their lives.

The living room was crowded with small and large items; beautiful fine china, layers of richly woven carpets, embroidered shawls, coloured glass, over embellished mirrors. If she had not been surrounded in those first weeks by the fittings in the house that she herself occupied and considered a prison, she would have thought she was in an alien world. On a visit one middle morning, she saw the table and sideboard laid out for the sister's meal, Amy noticed a pair of vine leaf shaped china dishes being filled with chutneys to accompany a platter of cold meats and commented on how she liked the colour blue, Elsa saw Amy's gaze linger on the two dishes,

'Pretty aren't they?' she said, 'strange curly top buildings and people on a little bridge and those two birds flying away, I like to think that's us flying away.' Elsa sighed, 'Stay, eat with us, you'll see they are the latest blue and white design called the Chinese Willow pattern. Cakebread brought them to us he said some Lord or other gave them to him.' Amy noticed by the look on Helen's face the woman was fighting to control something. She didn't have to wait long,

'He lifted them. You know he did.' She burst out.

'We said we wouldn't tell.' Elsa countered, 'I didn't like to say too much to-'

'To who, do you think she doesn't know he can't be trusted?' Helen parried, 'She's here in front of us?' indicating Amy with a lift of her chin, 'then don't let's treat her anything but family. She needs to know we are on her side.'

'Of course you're right dear.' Elsa agreed.

'What do you mean 'he lifted them'?' Amy asked.

'Oh darling girl,' Helen's tone was nothing but sympathetic, 'One time when he was bragging about his adventures into some Lord's pile.' Amy's face again showed she didn't understand,

'Pile ?' Amy enquired, her head tipped to one side, eye browsed raised questioningly.

'Ah yes, well he was showing off telling us about being in a Lord's castle, saying how he even sat and eaten at his Lordship's table, then, as he was following the old boy out of the dining room, he put his hand out and picked up these two vine leaf dishes off the Butler's board and slipped them in his pockets. He said, "The old Lord must have expected some excitement having riff raff the likes of me in his house, besides he'd got the kegs he'd wanted along with news of his brother in Paris, so I took a little extra 'evidence' on the side."

'Come along now eat with us, Elsa said, 'don't let's be afraid we must have some life outside his ugly regime.' Cluttered full of nick naks the house may have been, but being with Elsa and Helen was her little breathing space of freedom.

PREQUEL: 1765 – 1889

8

News

In the first letter back from Cleone; her only other sibling who Grandmother Shoesmith had encouraged to read and write, Amy learned that her mother and two sisters were no longer living at the house where they were born and grew up. Not long after Amy left their father had died. Tib told Cleone he had cut himself badly and was too stubborn to allow their mother to cleanse the wound, describing how a dark blood red vein bulged slowly up his arm. It killed him.

Their mother could not inherit the house so she and her two daughters had no home. Will and Liz Hartshorn came to their rescue by giving them one of their sheds between the carpentry shop and the Smithy to house the looms and equipment Eleanor determined were hers. She and the girls dismantled the means to make their livelihood, filling the wagon as if the loom parts were carpenter's offcuts, then started their journey just before dawn. It was only four miles through the pathways over to the Hartshorn's, but Eleanor judged it the fewer folks who knew their movements the better. Will allowed them to make a bedroom in the roof space above their workroom. He also sold the wagon and horse for them which made it possible to purchase their next year's stock of fleeces. They were all three very happy there.   Although no names or places were given in Cleone's letter nevertheless she had been able to convey their respective situations. No mention of grief. She was sad being cut off from her mother, sisters and Grandmother but she wouldn't miss her father.

As for Eleanor, Tibby and Tonia had told Cleone, she was a changed character, from being so servile in front of her husband, telling her daughters to keep their growing dislike of their Father's ways to themselves, their Mother was beginning to look like a woman they had never known; putting her hair up in a pretty knot, rolling her sleeves up above the elbow and fashioning a neat lace collar around the neck of her dress. 'He never loved me, your Father.' Eleanor told her daughters one day, although in her usual quiet gentle manner she added, 'I've always had nimble fingers he saw my use and took the opportunity for his own ends.'

Martha paused, her eyes and mind far away.

"My mother used to say Eleanor was just a slave, she had very few moments of her own to just to stand at the village well for a gossip. After that husband of hers went, she blossomed. "

9

Sally

When Amy was well on into her ninth month Cakebread returned from, she never knew where, with a woman whom he said was to look after Amy for the rest of her pregnancy and lying in, through the birth of his daughter and then oversee her full recovery. A daughter, Amy was surprised at the man's sureness.

Mrs Gillibert was kind and friendly but stern with Amy's routine sleep, rest and cleanliness. Amy had not been used to so much body washing.

Thankfully the baby was a daughter, she called her Sally. Cakebread was overjoyed – he knew he'd been right.

The baby needed for nothing. She had a wet nurse and a very separate Nursery. Mrs Gillibert, the laying in woman, stayed for a further week, 'to make sure,' she told Amy, 'that her milk was dried out.' Amy wanted to know why, when she thought the milk was needed for her baby. 'Well of course the sooner you can conceive again.' The woman replied huffily. A nursemaid took charge of Sally from then on and organised the wet nurse besides everything else.

The night of the day Mrs Gillibert left, Cakebread went straight back to his routine. She realised now he was hell bent on begetting children. And indeed she did, very soon become pregnant again, but unfortunately she lost the baby after only a few weeks and could not keep that from him for very long. Until two things dawned on her. Firstly, by telling him she had been sick that morning she knew he would not force himself on her again that night. Secondly, something now made sense; an item her grandmother Shoesmith passed on to women in the village market. At least, if she had to endure Cakebread's painful animal lusts, she could avoid any further pregnancies; her only problem was, having access to the garden and hedge rows close to the house; with Tilly in attendance was one thing, but she could not venture further afield. And, though she could smell the sea, she did not know how far away the seashore might be. She needed help to gather items other than those available in the countryside. Tilly was the one person she felt she could trust but she did not want to put the girl in danger by giving her too much information.

'Tilly, how far is the nearest pebble beach?' the girl looked surprised.

'Not far Madam.'

'How long would it take you to get there?' Amy enquired.

'A few steps,' the girl frowned. Amy showed her surprise. 'Just down the road apace.' Tilly offered.

'Would you fetch something for me please?'

'Surely I will Madam.' Tilly's Mother had told her daughter that she had come to the conclusion anything to do with the man Abel Cakebread was unholy. But he paid well, so we keep our mouths shut and do what we are asked. Tilly was not too sure she held with all he did, but she felt Amy was another matter, She would help her all she could.

'Would you have a look along the beach and collect me some pebbles with holes right through. Ones you can see through. I want to make a necklace like my Gran used to have; pebbles about the size of pullet's eggs.' Tilly began to wonder whether this request was for some kind of witchery. And was about to decline when Amy added, 'Remember, the size of pullet's eggs not pigeons, they would be too small; only when you've got time in the next few days.' Ah, now that made things better to Tilly's mind, because that night there would be a full moon and Mrs didn't want the gathering of the pebbles done on this night.

The baby turned into a beautiful child her natural movements were gentle and her skin delicately smooth, like a china doll. While Cakebread centred his attention on little Sally, Amy was fully aware he could throw her out at any time, but held on to the hope that since the wet nurse and maid had been dispensed with, he saw her as the best one to look after his child. Meanwhile, Amy was determined to see an opening for their escape as soon as safely possible, for that she would need some money of her own. Eleanor had outwardly, always seemed so bent to her husband's will until, as Amy now recalled she had cautioned her youngest daughter, just give love, never let your father's rebuffs crush you or you will be full of anger, like he is, be yourself. Keep strong. Again Amy decided it more prudent to think things through carefully.

PREQUEL: 1765 – 1889

10

Trade

Cakebread constantly urged Amy to dress in the clothes he had sent in to her. She never went anywhere to warrant such finery, but his will must be met.

"Dress everyday – look the lady, be proud, wear the face colouring and do up your hair. I want the child surrounded by well groomed women."

The hairdresser who attended Elsa and Helen now called in regularly to Amy. Amy got to know the woman well and soon started providing her with herbals and lotions. She thought it would keep her in tune with the needs of the hairdresser's wealthy clients; however Amy discovered women's needs didn't change much whatever their position in society. That bit of business the two women kept to themselves.

Frenchies

"Here wife take care of these." his voice called out late one night. Amy came hurrying down the stairs, just as the back door into the stable yard was closing. There seemed to be a heap of wet rags on the floor. A tiny whimper came from the rags. Holding her candle closer a small child's tear stained face came into view, the eyes as wide as saucers. The little body flinched sharply away when Amy put her hand out to wipe away the tears. Another slight movement revealed an even smaller child in fact there were four. She couldn't understand their tiny murmuring and not one would accompany her into the kitchen, so she took a clean cloth and a bowl of warmed water, set it down beside the children where they remained huddled together on the floor in the entrance passage, and proceeded to make a washing movement across her own face. It took her a long time to persuade the little mites into the kitchen but when they saw the fire she had built up in the grate the oldest one pulled the others to gather round and Amy was able to help them to drink some milk. It seemed to relieve some of the haunted look on their littles faces.

Meanwhile Amy's two new sisters gave her great support telling her that the children were French and that she shouldn't seek to learn anything about anybody who arrived in the house. They would not be there long. They knew what their brother was up to. They also knew Amy wasn't the only woman suffering. Sadly others were duped more than Amy. At least Amy had the comfort of the sisters but of course it wasn't enough.

Other quivering bundles of humanity arrived at intervals often in the night left inside the back door. Not always children. There were young adults both men and women, who wore rich clothing in different states of damage. None stayed very long, no longer than two or three days at the most. Amy came to know these frightened people could be very haughty in their fright, although most kissed her hands in thanks and relief. She was only able to help them clean themselves and provide a needed sustenance, before they were whisked away again. Witnessing him arrive to take these sad souls away, she saw Cakebread never showed them any kindness.

On one occasion she heard a low wailing coming from the cellar. It frightened her but the sound seemed so bleak she went to investigate all the same. A knife pierced her throat while a shaking hand pinned her against the wall. Amy felt the person was more frightened than she was; pushing gently at the man's chest she found he was so weak he almost fell over. This time a voice asked, in clear English,

"Who are you?" Amy learned from this man that he was French and fleeing from, "Peasants hell bent on murdering us all."

11

Conspiracy

From Sally's earliest days Helen and Elsa encouraged Amy to take their niece into the sea and teach her to swim. It was, they said, for the child's own protection. Fortunately Amy had learned, when quite a young child, to swim in the river where the family washed their fleeces. This was her first experience of the sea, but as she got to know more about the sisters' lives she could see the significance. Although she sensed they were still not telling her everything.

As soon as Sally was able to walk Cakebread insisted on taking his small daughter out on fishing trips. Amy had no say in the matter, whatever the man wanted to do, he did. The child had all the best clothes and protection. When on board she was roped for safety. Sally loved her trips, she loved her father. He was a kind and caring father to her. Elsa and Helen could see this and carefully said nothing against him in the hearing of the little girl. When she was only six years old Sally was already being dressed in outfits more fitting for adult women. The sisters could no longer stand aside in silence. They knew it would not be long before she would be used on the boat they worked on. They had held back long enough.

The three sisters in law talked over many things of their own experiences of life besides discussing how best to protect Sally for future events. It wasn't all sad or heavy talk; they often laughed at themselves singing and dancing around the room.

"Take no notice of me ladies," a smiling Cakebread had entered without a sound, "I'll just sit here – please go on, you are very entertaining. I won't interrupt." They didn't know how long he'd been there or even if he'd been standing listening outside the door. "Aren't you going to offer me a cup of our fine coffee? I know how good a quality it should be." "There he goes," – Helen said later, "Got to let us know who's paying for everything." It could go deeper than that passing snipe though. What had he overheard?

At this point Martha abruptly stopped and turned her head towards the door giving a small shudder, "I felt a waft of cold air." Then taking a deep breath she said, "It reminds me of Amy's very words. 'He wasn't just cruel, Cakebread, he was silently evil.' The girls had to think of every move before he did, be sharper than him"

Martha sighed and carried on, saying that all Helen and Elsa mentioned to Sally, in a very gentle way of course, that if she was ever asked to do anything she felt uncomfortable in doing on board one of Papa's boats, just to pretend to fall overboard, tread water to 'make as if you're drowning.' Sally was only a child, she was puzzled but agreed to do as her Aunties suggested. They knew Cakebread would never lose his little girl. He'd part the sea to save her. Sally mentioned her Aunt's suggestion to her mother one day. Amy held her counsel; she didn't want to frighten the child, so told her daughter to follow anything her Aunties said she should do. Still she could not believe she had herself been so duped, but how could she have known, she too had been an inexperienced child when she had been taken.

Amy finally did hear the whole story from her two sisters in law – all these years of their suffering, she was angry at being herself so used. Ah well that's what comes of being trained to be a dutiful daughter and wife – women were born to obey – she felt firmly that it wiped away any possibility she could ever love a man.

So there it was – all out in the open now. She heard how Cakebread had bullied his young sisters into looking over his second, 'fishing boat.' The cabins were astonishingly well appointed – two very small cabins – softly furnished and supplied with cut glass decanters and matching glasses. He took them out one warm summer's night. Candles in pink globes sent a shimmering haze inside each cabin. In mid-channel Cakebread's so-called fishermen on deck lit a set of especially coloured lanterns. A similar sequence of responding lights soon appeared nearby. A step ladder unfolded over the side and a well dressed man came aboard, being greeted with much deference by Cakebread. After a short whispered discussion, the guest was ushered below with a great show of deference and introduced to Elsa. Helen noticed gold changed

hands between mine host and the guest's servant, before the door
to her sister's cabin closed behind him. A short while later, looking
through her little round port hole, Helen saw another boat showed
its own set of lights before a second man boarded on her side of the
boat. Again the deference, but this time a bag of coins was handed
over. Helen had her first client. The women fared lightly that night,
only one client each.

"Do what you have to do," their brother had told them, "I need
them plient, there are things I want to know. If you can't do this for
me softly then I'll have to use a heavier hand my way." Whether it
was blackmail or spying; there must have been more to it than that,
considering the other cruel business he was conducting, made the
more-so that his sisters had to be involved for their very sustenance
and the roof over their heads.

As soon as the two visitors had made their separate departures,
the boat turned towards the lobster pots. Before the sisters had time
to fly to each other's arms and cry together, Cakebread pressed a
gold coin into the palm of each woman.

"You can have two each of these every night we come out here.
So think on before you scream at me. You know you've nowhere else
to go."

Trouble is he never did hand over any further coins, they were
so well guarded from that day on they had little opportunity to get
away.

The brother, who the two sisters only ever referred to by their
family name, Cakebread, had always been cruel and manipulative
through their childhood. As first born son he resented the
appearance of these twin sisters, who took their Father's attention
from him. Child, boy, man, in everything he did he aimed, and
meant to retain, the upper hand.

Early on in his youth he found ways to gather wealth and it
never mattered who he hurt in the process. When his father left him
the two fishing boats; one the Abel, he used for legitimate purposes
as a cover for the other, the Lucky Maid. Having, as he thought,
broken his sisters' will to his own, Cakebread set out to offer services
he knew would excite the new wealthy from the English side who
wanted to be leaders in their community and yet keep their special

requirements away from public sight. For the French he offered a dalliance as disguise for the exchange of information.

Helen learned early on what these very special services were from a sly client who offered her a better life and the opportunity to travel to Paris and Rome. Helen knew how to be evasive, not to commit herself and apparently not to understand, pretending her loyalty to her brother. It was lucky that she was so canny. From passed experience she guessed she would never see that man again and she was right. After leaving her cabin Cakebread treated the Frenchman with effusiveness plying him with brandies to loosen his tongue. She heard he died a few days later. Oh, nothing to do with the brandy drinks – no. The incident confirmed her suspicions that Cakebread had secret listening tubes into the two cabins and he had overheard the Frenchman's offer. Their brother was a mean man with no heart. The two girls kept up their silly women's chatter!

Amy learned the sisters were far from the silly women she had first encountered; seeing two overdressed bulge breasted females, hair crimped, faces rouged their ears bejewelled. When she got to know them the women turned out to be a strong and thoughtful, duo. The pair were little more than her own age; beautiful kind girls having their young lives sapped away. But they had not wasted their time. They'd learned to listen, when as children their father had taken them out fishing. Trade could be done mid channel, French spoken and learned. Their brother never suspected they understood what was being said, after all, they were only girls.

All in good time they'd make their move. Cakebread forgot they were of his own stock – persistent, determined – the very same brew but with the bit he lacked; sympathy and sensitivity.

Helen often saw a young fisherman on one of the boats that ferried the clients out from the French coast. She always managed to get up on deck for the fresh air. Cakebread was taken in when she said she wanted the air to bloom her skin. It was Elsa who, by chance discovered where their brother secreted his gold for which her twin formed another plan.

After she had satisfied her Client's desires – whatever it may be – she would gently cover his eyes with a feathery light slip of black velvet. Without exception every one of them fell into sleep once their needs were fulfilled. All commented on their experience to Cakebread himself, saying how refreshed they came from Helen's cabin.

Whilst it was she who pursued her own purpose, her client's short restorative slumbers gave her time to secrete her messages in the best spot in their waistcoat tails or greatcoats. Paul Moreau her fisherman lover by eye contact only, retrieved her messages, reciprocating back and forth. The clients had wealth that made them heedless of their clothing; they looked good but flung their clothes off with a sense of little value in material items being easily acquired. It's surprising what you can conceal in another man's waistcoat tails, unknown to its wearer. Her young fisherman was able to get his own boat with the money he made from the baubles gleaned from the clients. Some baubles cost a fortune although a passing fancy to the wealthy. Anyway these men had made themselves wealthy stealing from the rich titled ones running from the Revolution. And so, when the time was right, Helen and her lover to be knew the sequence of lights. Elsa knew the plan, she was happy to cover for her sister. Elsa had plans of her own but they had to hold back until the time was right to force his hand. They had to stop Cakebread. He could not be allowed to ruin any other woman's life especially a child's.

When the time was right, a third of the gold was removed and at the end of that night, Helen slipped quietly over the side as Cakebread gave orders to turn back to the English coast. Treading water she waited in silence awhile to give time for the boat to leave. Her Frenchman remained away in the darkness until it was safe for Helen to show a sheltered light. She was soon helped aboard and the pair sailed back to his home port, a wealthy couple.

Elsa said nothing keeping to her cabin feigning sleep. Back on shore she let the fishermen help her off the boat. Where was her sister? Oh I expect she still sleeps, was Elsa's answer, let her – she had more clients than I had last night. By mid-morning Cakebread, having been engrossed in grooming his small daughter, must have thought Helen had gone back up to the house without him seeing her leave the boat.

Elsa prepared herself for one of her brother's volcanic eruptions. He treated his sisters as his property, Business property. But he didn't come that day or the next. The weather kept the boats in the harbour. Elsa knew he would never believe she wasn't party to the conspiracy to get Helen away. When he found out she had gone there would be a furious row. Elsa kept her counsel. She told the maid to leave her sister to sleep, just for now. But the girl must have had her suspicions and any of the servants could tell Cakebread. After all he paid the piper.

The weather had to change and the routine would commence as usual. He hadn't got this far in life to be so easily tricked, whatever occurred Cakebread was ready with his own plans. On the third day, a calm day, sea like a millpond after the storm, Cakebread walked up from the harbour and straight past the sisters' house. Amy was ordered to get young Sally washed and dressed in the new outfit he had with him. He was taking his beautiful daughter on a very special journey.

Sally was excited. A new summer dress and ribbons for her hair.

'Can mother come too?' she asked her father.

''No, your mother is a poor sailor.'

It wasn't hard for Amy to know what he had in mind. She saw he stopped to fetch the sisters on his way to the boat, Sally skipping happily beside him in her new slippers and gown. At least the sisters would be with Sally. But she only saw Elsa come out to join her brother and niece. Cakebread walked on. Amy knew nothing of Helen's secret departure but when Tilly reported Miss Helen was 'sick' Amy knew the time had come to act. She had the rest of the afternoon and daylight hours. The boat would not return till morning unless something went wrong. As soon as she saw the boat leave on the high tide. Amy made her way on foot inland to meet the coach on the main road. She was well aware Cakebread could see her if she left the village on the pony and trap. To avoid recognition she borrowed Tilly's cloak. Using a path where a figure would be seen through a glass from the boat she walked like the young maid, swinging her basket like a child.

Amy didn't enter the village but met the stage coach out on the road after it had made its regular post stop. She quickly handed her two letters to the Post bag holder on the back so that nobody in the coach had time to see who hailed the coach, which then moved briskly on its way. She had sent letters, one each to her sisters at the Hartshorn's and the second to Cleone at Moat Mount. On her return across heath land she pulled a cotton bonnet over her hair and leaned heavily, like an old body, on a stick she had taken hidden in the folds of her cloak, stopping here and there, if she were seen it would look as if she was collecting herbs.

Should the worst happen and Sally needed to take to the sea she knew the child could swim like a fish in the sea, that part was an adventure to her daughter. She'd no doubt they would soon return if what the sisters expected, were to happen, so Amy had to set about her next task with some haste. Over the weeks she had prepared items in case she and her daughter needed to flee at short notice. Her plan was to tell Sally, they were having a holiday treat. Nevertheless, she was very careful.

With everything in place she sat down to her loom; the picture of a happy contented Mama at home at her leisure.

PREQUEL: 1765 – 1889

12

Escape

Sally had not been taken very far out to sea on the 'Lucky Maid' before. Excited was a mild indication of how the child was acting. Skipping in delight up the gangplank, nobody had to help her. Her father was proud of his sure footed little wench and in her childlike way she was proud to be with a strong man, now dressed in a sailor's manner, his luxurious hair sleekly waxed back and plaited into a tight queue.

"Are we collecting lobsters, Papa?"

"Yes, child what a clever girl you are."

"Well the deck's so clear. And you've got no nets or lines ready."

"Sharp eyed too, I see."

Sally had to look into everything. Pity she was wearing this silly dress and all these baubles. Aunty Elsa was dressed like this today too but she had gone straight down to her cabin. Her father's two crewmen weren't as fatherly friendly as the ones she was used to on the 'Abel,' but, well, they didn't know her and they were old enough to be her Grandfathers, although, of course she'd never known a Grandfather.

Dusk was closing in. Cakebread called his daughter down to see her cosy cabin. What a surprise she had, "It's like Aunty's boudoir at home." she giggled jumping on the piled up pink satin bed covers. "It bounces. Wee ee ee its fun."

"Do you like your cabin my lady?" asked her Father.

"Oh yes, happy happy. I should have brought Dolly Betty and Lamby toy." He left her to play while he went up on deck to set sail. Sally was too busy looking through all the small drawers and making faces at herself in the mirror, to notice the door click open. Turning, she saw a man in fine clothes standing looking at her.

"I don't know you," she said forthright, "I'm Sally, pleased to meet you."

She moved towards him, her hand outstretched to be kissed but he laughed,

"What a little madam you are." His comment made her frown because that was what her father had taught her to do, so therefore it was the right way, just good manners.

Taken aback by her frown he took her fingers to his lips but didn't let go, instead he pulled her onto his knee as he sat on the bed.

"What a pretty dress, don't you just look the lady."

"It's not very sensible for the sea." Sally replied.

"No, you're right. How does it come off? Let me help you. I expect your maid dresses you doesn't she?"

"No, my Mother's maid does and the skirt comes off easily, look."

"Well now, that is nice. Can you take those new fangled breeches off too?"

"No thank you Sir, I'm quite comfortable like I am." Sally looked at him as if he were a fool. His hand flashed out and tore at her clothes missing because he was too busy pulling at his own clothes.

Aunty Elsa's words tumbled into her mind, 'If you don't like what happens, get out'. Over the last few months Elsa had made more emphasis on the subject. And her final words had been, 'Don't hesitate.'

"I haven't got a mind for this sauce," the man was saying, "here ...." He didn't get time to finish his instructions. Sally, sure footed Sally, was out through the cabin door up on deck vomiting over the side before anybody could catch her.

Unfortunately for Cakebread the previously masked bully inside him was instantly exposed as he twisted about to see what the commotion was about.

"Stupid little bitch." he spat, "Blast! I should have locked that damned door."

It was out and she heard it. He didn't even have time to blink, before she was over the side and pretending to drown. He'd had no knowledge that she had been taught to swim; Amy could be far more devious than Cakebread would ever know. So he'd no idea the child was also acting out what she had been told.

While the crew were turning the boat towards her, for she was kicking herself away all the while flailing her arms and spewing out sea water, Cakebread was throwing a belt and line at the same time endeavouring to pacify the deeply irate visitor, trying to keep him calm.

A second visitor had arrived on the other side of the boat at the very moment Sally had burst from the cabin door. This man was laughing at the sight of a half clothed male heaving himself up from the cabin with his eager parts exposed.

Elsa could see from her tiny porthole how well the child was managing. She wasn't worried knowing Cakebread would never let the child drown; although all the while he was fighting to control a three-way situation in the evening light. "Bring the child inboard' he ordered his crew. "Get yourself back down in the dry man."

"What? What yer talking about man?"

"Just think," he almost said, DAMN YOU, but thought better of it, adding, "Wet, slippery, and a lovely fight you'll win."

Even Elsa told Helen later she was shocked to hear the cruel exploiter inside her brother selling his own child.

"Go below man – I'll deliver the prey back to you." Cakebread shouted again.

The man didn't move; not the brightest of men, he was still disappointed, a little winded and simply hungry for something he craved and couldn't let anybody else know about. The second man didn't move either, he remained bracing himself against the shrouds taking a draft from a silver flask watching events unfold, making no attempt to go below to Elsa's cabin.

Sally was hoisted out of the water dripping and shivering.

"Ah sweet thing, you need a warm." it wasn't her father speaking. The dishevelled man came towards her – arms open to enfold her. Stomach heaving Sally projectile vomited sea water all down the front of his dishevelled underwear.

"Well, if you will desire something so young you deserve all you get." the words of contempt came with a strong French accent, "Nubile is one thing but little children – yuk." he spat his gall onto the deck and with a shrill whistle he was over the side and back down into his own ship's dingy and gone.

"This is intolerable." growled the now totally deflated male, as he roughly pulled his coat closed around his slimy vomit splattered undergarments at the same time irritably hailing his ferry man. This was the one night Cakebread's usually carefully timed clients came together.

"No more of this, you'll not see me again." Cakebread's urging made no sense now. In all the argy-bargy Sally had run unnoticed down into Elsa's cabin.

The 'Lucky Maid' was ordered to make for the shore.

A rough scuffling, door crashing back against its hinges before midnight, announced Sally's return, the little girl was pushed into the hall, a voice above her head shouting to Amy,

"Clean the child up." The door banged shut. Then they heard his horse urged noisily out of the yard. The man's anger was audible through the violent sliding clatter of metal shod horse's hooves on the cobblestones.

The child stood bare foot in the hallway, an old blanket round her shoulders, hair stuck wet cross her face. In the candle light Sally's ivory white face looked stunned as if made of wax.

"Oh dear sweetheart let's get you a warm bath." Peeling away the blanket Amy saw the bruises, there was little left of torn cotton underwear. Amy was hardly able to contain her shock. Her eyes must have said it all but she had resolved not to say anything, not to ask questions now it would only make it worse for the child.

Standing Sally in a bowl of warm water Amy wrapped a soft fireside dried towel round the child's body whilst she gently sponged her down removing the ripped bits of garment under the towel as she sponged.

Lifting her daughter out of the water she sat her on her lap gently drying one foot at a time. As the child's rigour subsided, tears began to flow slowly at first then as the ordeal returned to her visual memory the crying changed to hot frightened horror and words, words – "W-worse than the Aunties had said. Man had wiggley animal in his pocket. – I jumped into the water. - kicked my shoes off 'cos they were too heavy." Her words came hiccoughing and stuttering out now.

"What a sensible girl you are." Amy answered.

"It was better in the water, safer. - Papa said terrible things – his face – hating looks – there was a Frenchman he laughed but he was angry really. - Papa swore at Aunty Elsa and hit her. He locked me in on my own."

All the while Amy dried the child and put her in a nightgown then into her own bed that Tilly had warmed with a warming pan. Amy got in beside her daughter making quieting sounds.

"It's all over now sweeting. I wouldn't have let you go if I had known." The last thing the child said before she went to sleep was, "You couldn't have stopped him Mamma."

Well before dawn Amy met Elsa at the back door to the stable yard. They decided to go ahead with their plan immediately.

"Here take this," Elsa put a small parcel into Amy's hands, "just a little something to remember us by lest we never meet again. Is Sally alright?" Amy nodded. "I'm leaving now. Harry's prepared a horse for you and Sally. He'll stay until you leave. Make it soon, before dawn dear."

"What about you Elsa you won't be travelling alone will you?"

"No Harry will catch up with me near Dover. He says Cakebread's taken his long distance horse, but don't be fooled he's doubled back before to catch us all out."

"Yes, you're right. We'll be ready in the quarter hour." The two women embraced. Communications had been planned.

"Good luck safe journey."

Amy told Sally she was taking her to see a doctor before they go for a holiday. Another necessary lie in case they should have the misfortune of being caught by Cakebread.

PREQUEL: 1765 – 1889

13

The Journey

Amy had known for some time where Cakebread put his stash of gold in the house. She'd told Helen and Elsa, who both said she should take it. Teach him a lesson. But Amy said no, she would only take what she had saved of the monies he had left her on the dressing table. The sisters were taking their share from the money Helen had discovered – well, that's what they had earned. It was quite obvious that he had meant the women to find the bundles of money he had planted.

"If I take that money from his hiding place he'd never ever stop looking for me, it was dirty money from his dirty business and all the smuggling."

Like the writing paper in his desk he never used it, that was another lure just to catch her out and it hadn't worked.

Amy and Sally were away well before sun up. Harry led their horse quietly out of the stable yard and followed behind up over the hills away from the village across to the road north where he left them taking care not to let Sally see him change his direction, turning east towards his rendezvous with Elsa.

Through byways and lanes, watching the sun Amy found the village where her mother and sisters were living and skirted round to Will Hartshorn's carpenters shop, waiting to make certain he had no customers before she made her entry.

Eleanor and her daughters had been expecting Amy any day and were overjoyed to see her again after all these years. It was the first time they had met Sally. Nevertheless quiet was kept. Will unpacked the horse's panniers, gave the animal a feed and water then led her away from the village well down a trail westward, leaving saddle and bridle as if the rider had fallen.

"She will wander her way back towards the smell of the sea," Amy said, "she's not mine and I don't want her presence to give us all away."

The plan had to run its full course. Eleanor, Tibby and Tonia were sad their visit was so short, but everyone knew the fanatical determination of the persuer they were dealing with. The next day Amy and Sally picked up the London coach for Canterbury then left it well before the City where they sat on the side of the lane to eat the food Eleanor had packed for them.

Filled with happy expectancy mother and daughter quickly walked away North-West this time, Sally skipping this way and that, picking flowers and all chatter. Cleone had written clear guidance so that by early evening Amy saw a familiar figure walking up the lane towards them.

"Hallo there."

"Mama, how did Granma Eleanor get here before us?"

"It's not your Granma darling it's Cleone, my sister, your other Aunty." All three ran towards each other and met in a huddle of laughter, mingled with Amy's tears.

Sally chatted away to Cleone telling her all about their journey. The two women couldn't get a word in. As Cleone led them along pathways, just wide enough to give way to a farm cart and through wooded hollows beside fields, Sally wanted to know all about the holiday they would be having; 'oh,' and where would they sleep this night? It was all so exciting, Cleone had to ease herself in front of the two travellers to slow their pace; they had hardly noticed the ground ahead was sloping down into a deep valley. In the gathering dusk Sally quietened at the sight of a lovely old mellow stone building set on a low hill with lights twinkling through a great end window. Through the small glass panes a many branched antler candelabrum shed sparkling light from an array of candles; more candles than Amy and Sally had seen in their lives. As they walked across the bridge toward a small door at the rear of the house Sally noticed the cool air rising from the moat surrounding the building; on hearing clucking sounds from below, the little girl ran to the wall at the side of the bridge, in the fading light she could just see a family of ducks settling their babies for the night; deep quaking calls caused her to look up at a skein of wild geese passing over head. Cleone smiled at the child's delight as she gently laid a calming hand on her young niece's shoulder,

"See right up the top of that tower there," Cleone pointed to a small candlelit window just under a tiled roof above a beamed overhang, "that's our bedroom."

Sally squealed with delight. Amy and her sister laughed at the child who had walked miles that day and was still running hither and thither.

"She'll sleep on a pin tonight." Cleone laughed.

"Oh lovely, that's just what Mum used to say when we got back from the market. I'm so glad to be with you Cleo." The two sisters put their arms round each other's waists as they took the last steps along the bridge to the door.

Sally slept for almost twenty-four hours.

Cleone had told Amy about their housekeeper. "Mrs Mountjoy will see you this afternoon. We need help with spinning the wool this season, Lady Lavender has taken to weaving so there should be work for you for a few months. She said the family will want a young nursery maid, I know Sally is very young but the child in need of a maid and companion is also very young."

"Do the family have traders calling? Amy asked.

"No need to worry my love few people come this way – it's too far off the beaten track. Only invited guests come here to Moat Mount."

PREQUEL: 1765 – 1889

14

Cat and Mouse

It was eight months before Amy heard that Cakebread had turned up at the Blacksmith's next door to the Hartshorn's carpentry shop. Tom Hartshorn, Will and Liz's son, noticed the great black horse being shoed by the village Farrier earlier in the day, so it was unusual to see the animal tethered at the edge of a nearby spinney late in the evening, it made him stop and look to see where the rider was.

Almost immediately he caught sight of a man's shape moving silently round the back of the sheds but before confronting the furtive looking figure he went swiftly round to where he attracted his father's attention and beckoned him from the workshop. Each going silently in opposite directions they came upon the black horse's owner peering into the side of the weavers' workshop, where he could see Eleanor working in the candle light.

"Good evening Sir." Will spoke first, looking directly into Cakebread's face.

Cakebread shouldn't have been surprised, but he must have been getting slovenly, it being only a month previously that he had lost his women and the credibility that brought the greater part of his livelihood. Even those who would not have believed he was a bully had heard different, and had their minds changed by well placed men who had sown the seeds of doubt. Business trust lost and still no sign of the women's whereabouts, both Will and Tom knew Cakebread would be more dangerous.

"I'm looking for my wife Amy and my daughter. I see her mother is here."

Hearing the man's tone Tom sought to defuse the atmosphere saying,

"Well my goodness Amy. Aw, haven't seen Amy Mortain for years."

Will knocked on the door and walked into the weavers' workshop.

"Mrs Mortain, there's a gentleman outside asking for Amy." Eleanor caught her shuttle and held its return journey before turning,

"Oh my dear we haven't seen our Amy for some years now. Who is it? Tell him he can come in." a wink and a raised eyebrow had passed between Will and Eleanor.

"Come in sir." Will Hartshorn kept his position in the doorway. Cakebread had to sidle in past him.

"Oh, good evening Mr Cakebread." Eleanor showed surprise as she stood up to face Cakebread.

"Has my wife been here Mrs Mortain?"

"No sir. I have not seen her since the day you rode away with her all those years ago," then her expression changed and she looked extremely agitated, "I hope my daughter is well sir, you worry me."

"Very well thank you Mrs Mortain. Did you know we have a child?"

"No sir." Eleanor smiled brightly at him, "How wonderful, congratulations. How old is the child sir?" No, he was not going to catch her out.

"Thank you, the girl is well." Terse as ever Cakebread turned to go. He didn't see Tibby and Tonia, they stayed out of sight the man could not be trusted.

He went away but he didn't go away. He was noticed for some weeks watching from a distance. They got on with their daily routines and watched him watching them. Two months went by in this cat and mouse situation. Then one day he wasn't there anymore.

15

A time of tranquility

Living at Moat Mount was such a tranquil experience for Amy. From her earliest years she had been made to sit long hours at the loom. Right up until she was fifteen, Amy's life had been relentlessly hard. Every hour of daylight she had worked at wool preparation, weaving and sewing. It was the only way she knew. Since being in the service of the Lavender's household she was experiencing other people's family lives and realising just how much her own father had been a tyrant with his constant harshness; driving her mother, her sisters and herself into working long hours with never a word of kindness. He had kept all the earnings from their weaving, saying they had a roof over their heads and food, they should be satisfied with that.

She didn't want to even think of the years with Cakebread and his bullying bestiality. His sisters were a little island of support, had it not been for them she felt she would have gone under.

At Moat Mount she enjoyed the few hours teaching Lady Lavender to spin and weave; then showing the waiting women how to finish off their mistresses work. Cleone had been right, only invited guests came to the Mount and they were dignitaries of the church and politicians. Sometimes royal personages made brief private visits.

The best times were when she and Cleone had their hours of freedom; when together they walked in the great parkland or sat quietly sewing in the servant's sitting-room or out in the gardens. Amy made pretty dresses for Sally and little Suzanne, who Sally had been engaged to befriend and nursemaid. Lord and Lady Lavender kept Suzanne away in her own apartments out of sight; only a very few family or servants even knew she existed, for when the Lavender's youngest child was born she was immediately put into a set of hastily prepared nursery rooms, far from the main family wing. It seemed everybody in the house was gagged, for the little girl had a difference.

Lady Lavender could not forgive herself for bearing such an aberration.

Her Ladyship was so kind to Amy and always pleased about everything she was learning; from the colour making to dyeing fleeces, to spinning the wool. For a while the two women had the kind of rapport only generated with a personal lady in waiting and her mistress.

Sally had already taken up her place in the nursery wing where at first she shared a room for sleeping with the nursemaids. But then, after the wet nurse departed when the babe was two years old, and that time Sally although still so young, just coming up for eight she became the baby girl's only human contact. After Amy had taught Lady Lavender to use the loom her husband bought for his wife, his Lordship said Amy should return to her family.

Only she and Cleone knew it wasn't safe for Sally to go back to the Hartshorn's because the family had sent warning of Cakebread's visit and still nobody was sure where he was.

Amy need not have worried as young Sally was only too happy to stay with baby Suzanne Lavender. Of course Lady Lavender could not have been more delighted and relieved to have the child remain as companion nurse.

Naturally Amy was sad to leave her daughter, but the little girl's position was safer at Moat Mount, especially as Cleone was in the same house. Amy would have to face her own situation.

Back again with her Mother and sisters Amy had her own small loom up above the shed where the three women worked. Nobody could be absolutely certain of their secrecy if Cakebread returned and found Amy, so it was safety first. She would keep out of sight as far as possible.

By this time Helen and Elsa were both well established in France and each keeping in touch with Amy through the Hartshorn's and although they knew where Sally was, communications were only ever made through the Hartshorn family and never directly by their own names.

A letter arrived from France with news. Elsa said she would hold nothing back. They had been informed that Cakebread's bird pecked body had been washed up on a beach on the Atlantic coast, his throat had been cut and the Lucky Maid was beached and gutted by fire further along the coast. She further explained that along with the information, she had received a package; the writer adding, that the contents would no doubt be of interest to the sisters. No mention was made of Amy. The package contained a lock of black hair and a blood caked severed thumb still wearing the ugly thumb ring with which he had used to hurt them all, at one time or another. That ring had certainly left a scar on Amy's ankle that turned out to be a lifetime's memory.

When that news had reached the Hartshorn's, six months after the sisters had first received it, the ever present veil of fear was lifted from the whole family, none more than Amy herself of course. Now she was able to release the cold nagging nugget of worry that clung deep down in the pit of her being.

Finally Amy was liberated from the ever present ghost of the man, who could still have turned up to claim that he owned her.

PREQUEL: 1765 – 1889

16

Relief and Joy

Amy gradually became aware she was awake, her half dream half waking state cleared. Her bed space was flooded with sun light through a small window in the roof of the barn and she could hear the birds chirruping in full throat; their calls telling her it was their dawn chorus. A warm blissful feeling filled her body.

Last night Tom had asked her to marry him.

Dear Tom, so hesitant; no sooner had he asked than he added,

"If you don't want to Amy, just say. I'll understand I really will." She'd wanted to answer him straight away but he quieted her, saying, "No, now you just go up to your bed and think it over." With that he'd opened the workshop entrance, handed her gently inside and quietly closed the door behind her.

As early as the hour was, in the room below the looms were full of rhythmic industry, clat clopping, clat clopping and Tibby's low voice came up through the trap door singing her usual morning song. Amy's thoughts worked their way back across such a happy time at Moat Mount when she shared the servants' bedroom up in the tower with Cleone and the other maids who sang their own morning chorus.

On returning to her Mother and sisters at the Hartshorn's, she had found Tom, the Hartshorn's son, living back at the family home, his young wife Molly had died in childbirth not long after she and Sally had made their short stop at her Mother's weaver's loft above the Carpenter's shop, on their way to Moat Mount. Tom had brought his baby son George, who was now being loved and cared for by his grandmother, Liz and three doting Aunties, Eleanor and Amy's two sisters.

Tom grieved long and deeply for the loss of his young wife but over the months with the return of Amy his mood had softened. He was very relaxed, working back in the Carpenters with his father and all the family round him. He and Amy had a lot in common to talk and commiserate about, he often walked protectively alongside her across the fields and woodland at dusk or early in the mornings as she collected herbs, because then she still wasn't entirely free. Amy said Tom Hartshorn was completely different to the two men she had known in her early years; each of those men had carried so much hate inside them.

Dear, sweet tempered Tom was a strong quiet character so kind and thoughtful; when she said she would prefer to follow her skills and knowledge of herbal remedies instead of working at the loom, he encouraged her to do what was most fulfilling, saying, if she enjoyed what she was doing then that is what she would do best. In return, she said it thrilled her to be his helpmeet.

Their marriage would be built on respect and honour each being well aware of their past sad experiences and each proud of the skills they brought to their partnership.

It was some months before they consummated their union. Tom had loved his young wife Molly so very deeply. She had given him a beautiful boy losing her own life in the process.

In her turn Amy found it extremely difficult to give herself freely to any hand after the repellent physical experiences she had undergone. Quiet closeness was their comfort. Tom was so careful not to touch her intimately at first especially when memories of his wife rushed in on his thoughts. Many nights he cried himself to sleep in his new wife's arms. His sadness was heartbreaking. Neither yet could Amy fully give of herself. They were patient one with the other

Tom took Amy and George in his father, Will Hartshorn's two horse cart, on a journey across country to Moat Mount so that he could meet Sally and Sally meet her step-brother George; such a dear little boy then nearly two years old. He called Amy Mummy from the start – well, he'd never known his Mother. Amy loved and cared for Tom's baby as her own. It was such a joyful time especially made the more so when Sally was allowed to join the family as they travelled on to stay for a few days with Cleone and Albert, her new stonemason husband, at their home in Canterbury.

With the family all being together that summer the tensions of their past were broken. Tom and Amy made love in joy and tears of happiness giving them James followed in the next four years by Edwin and Joseph.

Outside a church yard on Romney Marsh sits a small memorial stone, resting back low against the flint wall, it bears the words –

Helen and Elsa in loving memory.

It is said the stone was placed there little more than a week or so after the two women disappeared. It's not known who put it there.

PREQUEL: 1765 – 1889

17

The life of letters

Since leaving Lady Lavender's service Amy wrote a letter to her daughter every month. As Sally became confident with her writing she placed a reply on the hall table, along with the family letters that were taken to meet the regular post chase. So, it was that Mother and daughter began, each to exchange their newsy correspondences on alternate months; a written conversation that lasted for the rest of their lives. Amy's in the hand of formal lettering she had, with her Grandma Shoesmith's guidance, partly taught herself from the Decalogue on the wall of their village church; and Sally's in the cursive hand she learned to write under the tuition of the older Lavender children's priestly tutor. From her earliest days at Moat Mount Sally, attracted by the colourfully painted ceiling in the family chapel, had attended daily prayers sitting at the back with Cleone in the servants' boxes; the priest noticed the little girl often stayed back at the end of the service carefully outlining words, with her finger, in the prayer book; always taking an opportunity to ask questions, showing far more interested to learn than the Lavender children. With the encouragement of her Aunt Cleone, Sally learned that the way to knowledge was to learn to read. To the priest she was such an engaging child, waiting behind after prayers, asking how to write down this word; what is the meaning of this sentence? Sally wanted to know about all sorts of subjects. So quick to learn she was a joy for the enthusiastic young teacher, who had become rather disillusioned by the almost complete indifference of the Lavender children, with what he hoped would be a rewarding position in such an internationally influential man's household. It was therefore Sally who reaped the benefit. Early one morning, when he, taking advantage of the sun's angle onto the writing slope in his small cubbyhole, he became aware of a slight movement behind his shoulder; he was enchanted to find the child was watching. Not wishing to frighten her, he completed the line in his beautiful flowing hand, finishing with his usual intake of breath hearing the child and he had exhaled in unison. It surprised him to know she had held her breath with his progress. No, astonished him that one so young was already aware of the discipline it takes to write a steady hand. But then surprised him yet again by remarking how sensible his sleeveless jacket was. 'My jacket?' he'd enquired, 'Why yes, no sleeves to impede your writing arm Sir.' Maybe he was flattered at her interest; maybe it gave him hope, boosted his ego; made him feel good at being teacher after all. The Lavender children never showed any further interest after their planned lesson times with him. He knew there were very young children in the house but had no further knowledge of to whom they belonged, he imagined it was Mrs Mountjoy, the housekeeper. What he did have was an uncanny feeling that this child would one day be a very valuable member of society, maybe more than those who were born to privilege. Thereafter, he was glad to show her how to cut a quill, quick to let her take over at her insistence, and frequently giving her spare edges of vellum for her practice. To Sally, all this was so she would also have a quill and bits of vellum for the friend of whom he had no knowledge at all. For her part, Sally reasoned it was she who would have to be Suzannah's teacher. The parents made no provision to educate the child; a child she knew to be very bright. While Amy was still at Moat Mount helping Lady Lavender with her weaving, she had brought small shanks of coloured wools for the girls to work samplers, setting them on a regular routine including letters and numbers into their picture making. From this small beginning Suzannah proved herself to be quick and eager to learn. In one letter to her Mother, Sally described herself and Suze as, 'A pair together, we enjoy being busy.'

One morning Tom came in from the workshop saying the local carrier had brought a letter from Sally, rather sooner that month than Amy would have expected; but what was unusual was the message the carrier left with Tom, which was that he would be passing back through the village the next day and had been asked to collect an answer. In her letter Sally asked her Mother to write to Lady Lavender with a special request that she, Sally, could be allowed home to help Amy manage through a family bereavement.

Amy was fully aware of the situation with Sally's young charge Suzanne Lavender and supposed there might be trouble brewing in that direction. So, without delay she wrote a friendly letter to her Ladyship with the request, as her daughter had asked. When Sally arrived at the Hartshorn's, it was her very first visit to her Mother and Tom's home and her first meeting with her new brothers, small James and baby Edwin.

While sitting with Amy, who was hastily patching the little boy's bloomers, Sally told her Mother the whole story that required her hurried departure from Suzannah and Moat Mount.

Most of the company around the inglenook had been staring dreamily into the fire as they listened to Martha's story, until her silence brought them all to attention with an intake of breath as if coming round from a sleep. But no, all eyes were wide open and waiting for Aunt Martha to go on.

"Nobody in the village had known about Amy and Sally stopping overnight that time they were in flight from Cakebread. So this was the first time I met Sally. Since Amy had returned to work with her mother and sisters, then married Tom and set up their own family home in the village she and I had once again rekindled our old close girlhood friendship. Sally was everything her mother had talked about; a lovely caring girl. Not very tall, but not petite; she had beautiful skin reminding me of Amy when she was young. It was when Amy and I sat sewing in the afternoons that we heard what turned the paths of Sally's and Suzannah's lives and how I'm able to tell you their story now.

PREQUEL: 1765 – 1889

18

Sally's story, Moat Mount, Kent

Nine year old Suzanne Lavender sat in a secluded corner of the kitchen garden reading aloud to her nursemaid, Sally Hartshorn. A natural born artist, Sally was making a water colour study of a tall fluffy purple artichoke head, while Suzanne read from a small, leather bound book, the names of the insects that helped clear white fly from the vegetables.

The morning was sunny and very warm. Sally looked up to see why Suzanne had stopped reading. Measured footfalls could be heard drawing closer, crunching along the gravel path the other side of the high box hedge that sheltered the north side of the vegetable garden. Two people, a man's and woman's voices spoke quietly as they moved into the seated alcove; one of the secret nooks set into hedges around the grounds known as trysting spots. Their conversation sounded more conspiratorial than romantic, the woman seemed agitated.

"Are you sure Johan, can you do this. I mean can you really remove an eye?" she questioned.

"I know, I haven't performed this operation before but it would be so useful to my research and helpful for my paper to the Society. I must take this opportunity."

"But she is just a child. If it goes wrong she could be disfigured for the rest of her life. And – would she not lose the sight in that eye?"

"It is not known if there is any sight in the eye. It is what her father wants Beatrice, and best performed before she is ten years old. Plenty of time for her to get used to a glass insert and it will heal before she is a young woman."

"Have you seen the child, does she want this done?"

"No I haven't and the choice is not hers. The father wants it."

"Well, if you are sure."

"I have suggested to her father the child could learn to speak German; she would then be an asset to his political friendships and you would be ideal as her governess Beatrice. Then, come the time, you can be here to tend her for me."

"Yes I am a nurse, but I'm not a teacher, I only know a little of your language and I can't get away yet Johan."

"No, I realise my dear. That's why I've said I will return in a month to carry out the operation, to give the family time to make their preparations with the child. I do need to do more reading about the eyes before then." The pair walked on.

As she listened to the progress of the conversation Suzanne pressed her hands against her mouth to stifle any sound. In that moment the horror of the implications brought huge tears into her eyes. Sally, at first struck dumb, speedily gathered herself. She was horrified to see the stricken look on Suzannah's poor little face.

"Suze," she whispered urgently, "nobody must know you and I have heard this conversation. Recover yourself sweetheart." Suzanne, taking a deep breath looked up at Sally and gave her a wry smile and relaxed. Although very young she couldn't fail to see the unintended humour in Sally's warning, for Suzanne never had contact with other persons to whom she could pass on any subject. Without delay the little girl replaced the eye-patch she had removed while she was reading.

In all her years Suzanne had been forced to stay away from other people, even her own brothers and sisters. She was well acquainted with smothering her feelings. Crouching closer to her young charge, Sally whispered,

"We must act sooner than we planned. Are you ready sweetheart?"

Suzanne nodded her agreement.

A day or two before this revelation, Sally had been lending an extra hand in the kitchens as the family were receiving important visitors from London. One of the parlour maids came downstairs saying a foreign sounding gentleman was entertaining the company with histories about people's eyes. Her words made Sally prick up her ears because the maid, who was one of the elderly members of the household who had lived at Moat Mount since she was a young maid, went on further to say that she'd heard Sir Hugh admonishing his wife for being stubborn, if she persisted in objecting to getting something done about their daughter's predicament, the girl would never land a suitable husband with such an eye.

Sally's eldest sister, Cleone had been a seamstress in the sewing room at Moat Mount sometime before Lady Lavender gave birth to Suzanne. The serving girls, at the time, had whispered about her Ladyship never forgiving herself, and even after all this time, still berated herself to her husband for bringing forth such a defective child. From the day of her birth the little girl had been kept secreted away from the family and servants. Lady Lavender came to Suzanne's rooms rarely and always knocked on the door calling to the nursemaid, 'Is the child covered?' before she would enter. A small black patch covered the defective eye before her Mother would hardly turn her face toward what she called her 'aberration'. Even then she hardly looked at her small daughter, it totally escaped her notice how the little girl grew in beauty or of Suzanne's lithe graceful movements, when coming forward to proudly show her Mother her handwork.

Sally could see the child's wistful looks as she watched out of her window, high up in the tower, her brothers and sisters at their play down in the gardens, sometimes being joined in their games by friends and later their sweethearts. Recently, her eldest sister was walking more sedately on the arm of the chosen partner. In fact Sally had written in her last letter home to her Mother Amy, how Suzanne was growing far more attractive than any of the older Lavender children.

Sally knew Suzanne would have little chance to love and be loved in the natural way like her siblings and now, the father was saying, it wouldn't happen at all without a dangerous operation that could easily go wrong.

Sally, who had changed her name to Hartshorn when her Mother remarried, was herself no stranger to flight from parental cruelty.

Although she had no personal knowledge of a world outside Moat Mount, Suzanne understood what had to be done to get away from her life that was no life. Their plans were prepared and were now put into operation. A note sent to Sally's mother, Amy, now Mrs Harsthorn, brought a letter to Lady Lavender requesting Sally's annual one week leave be brought forward to allow her to come home immediately as she desperately needed her daughter's help as there had been a sudden death in the family. Lady Lavender remembered Amy with affection and so being a kind employer to her servants readily agreed. Sally packed her bag and left. Lady Lavender instructed her own personal maid, Bebe, to see that Suzanne's food and clothing were left in the anteroom to the child's chambers for the period Sally was to be absent. This plan suited the pair's plans nicely Sally and Suzanne knew how much pressure Bebe was under to keep her Mistress served, without this extra responsibility.

The following evening, after Sally departed on the stage coach, apparently towards her home, Suzanne went for her regular walk in the gardens. Bebe knew about this usual walk to catch the fresh air before bed time; it was dark nobody would see her and at nine years old Bebe felt Suzanne could take the walk alone.

Taking her usual pathway around the woodland edge of the grounds, Sally had warned her not to carry anything with her, lest she was seen and it reported she could be running away. In the smoky brown twilight at the far edge of the garden, a low whistle told Suzanne that Sally's sister Cleone was waiting in the shadows. In the years Cleone worked for the Lavender's at Moat Mount she knew the lay of the land very well. Taking Suzanne's hand the pair walked a mile away from the estate before they came upon a sheltered glade where Cleone's husband was waiting with a pair of horses. Cleone and Albert, with Suzanne up behind him, rode swiftly to Canterbury where Sally was waiting at their cottage near the Cathedral.

Sally had brought Suzanne's small bag of clothing, in fact all she would have to take to her new life. The child was so excited having never been further than the garden boundary to the Moat Mount estate.

"Now darling, remember you will not see me for a while." Sally reminded Suzanne. "Go with Cleone and Albert. They will travel with you to my Aunt Helen across the water. She and her husband Paul will take great care of you. Have no worries. I will be with you as soon as it is safe."

"Bye bye Sally. I do love you." The child clung to the only human being who had ever given her love and comfort.

"Bye sweetheart."

While Sally took a coach back to the Hartshorn's family Carpenter's, south into Sussex the following day, Cleone and Albert journeyed with Suzanne to Dover and across the Channel to France.

PREQUEL: 1765 – 1889

19

A child who had not existed until she disappeared

As luck would have it Suzanne's breakfast wasn't left for her as arranged because Bebe was just too busy to check, and the kitchen hadn't normally made meals for the little known child, Sally usually did everything upstairs in their wing of the house. Therefore no food arrived until later that day when a laundry maid left the tray beside the clean clothes outside the door. Not only that, but it wasn't until cook noticed food she had put on a tray for an evening meal had not been taken up to the child.

'Here lad,' she caught one of the kitchen boys, 'find y'er way up to where Sally works. That child must be famished by now.' Some of the older servants did know about Suzanne and were able to show the young man the way. When the same lad went up to collect the tray the next morning the food had not been touched.

'Oh my goodness Bebe will be in trouble.' Cook sighed, 'She's supposed to be looking after the child while Sally's away. Can't tell 'er til she gets down 'ere for 'er supper.'

Therefore the knowledge that the child wasn't eating was even further delayed until Bebe came down to the servants' room much later, after Lady Lavender had finally dismissed her. When she did come it was at such a speed and haste that all she could say was, 'Oh, 'spect she's just sulkin'. Leave the food she'll eat it if she's hungry. Oh dear, Lady L. forgot about all the extra visitors we're receiving this week; it's change into this dress, now get that hat ready or I'll wear that wig; no, I must change again for bloomin, 'wotsiself's visit; all these extra changes of clothes, I'm fair frazzled.' Bebe's complaining went on and on all the while she was shovelling food in her mouth and swigging a drink. 'What with 'er Ladyship up one end o' the 'ouse, and the child up the other. Just leave the food outside, do ...' she called over her shoulder as she grabbed a clean overall on her way through the laundry room.

The food was still untouched three days later.

At last Cook told Bebe she would have to go to investigate and of course her Ladyship's maid found no sign of the child in her apartments at all. Suzanne was nowhere to be found. Lady Lavender had to be told. Bebe heard from one of the kitchen maids that she had seen the little girl leaving through a side gate into the garden for her walk but couldn't remember which evening it was.

Sir Hugh did not hear about the child's disappearance until he returned from an important state meeting. By then there had been no sighting for a week. He questioned the servants himself and sent all the young lads to go around the grounds to call the child's name. In the midst of the uproar Sally alighted from a local carrier's cart in the lane and was walking in through the gate to the kitchen yard when a stable boy caught sight of her and a kitchen maid rushed to tell her the child was missing. Sally stood still staring in disbelief. She dropped her bag on the cobbles and stood there, aghast at what they were telling her,

'She hasn't been eating you say?'

'Nah, nuffin, so cook says' squawked a naive young scullery girl.

Sally couldn't take in all the gabbled words. Already seven days and nights had gone by since she left to visit her family.

'P'raps she's playin' hide'n'seek' spoke a young groom.

'Silly.' a group of voices replied.

'Oh dear maybe she's fallen and is hurt' Sally mouthed, tears coming to her eyes. 'I'll go to all her favourite spots.' Leaving her bag where she'd dropped it Sally began to run, some followed her to help. Bebe let Lady Lavender know of Sally's return.

Sir Hugh was in the chamber with his wife when Sally arrived back from her search. The air was volcanic. He was raging how when he was so busy with affairs of state blasted women went and got themselves lost. 'Damn females, can't look after anything,' he was shouting and just at a time he had important visitors to host. High officials, men who were passing through Kent would be calling in at Moat Mount on their way to King George's Court any day. His official duties most certainly had to be kept apart from family affairs. Angry as he was he was forced by his station in society to keep this particular matter secret, 'Blast and damnation, if women could only make up their minds all this could have been avoided'. The house steward was sent to carry out a discrete investigation around the area. The child seemed to have totally disappeared. Naturally little information could be broadcast because nobody in the surrounding countryside knew Sir Hugh even had another daughter. Lady Lavender certainly didn't want it known in society that the little girl's face was disfigured.

For weeks the household went about their business under a heavy cloud lurking around their ears; nobody knowing who to point a finger at, or which way to turn to find this lost child; a child who hadn't existed until she disappeared. Gradually, and inevitably, all momentum fizzled out of the search. With no reason for her being part of the household any longer Sally was sent for and stood, fighting back her tears, before Lady Lavender.

'You should not have left the child for a week' she rebuked the nursemaid. 'For that I shall dismiss you.' Then Sally did cry, but quietly. 'Sir Hugh will not countenance you being here any longer.' Lady Lavender pronounced, hiding behind her husband's will. Nevertheless she weakened sending a small envelope by Bebe to Sally containing the fare money to cover her journey home. At least Bebe hadn't been dismissed. It hadn't been her fault Suzanne had to flee. Although Sally had hoped for her own wage paid up to date, at least she wasn't accused of the child's abduction. She was free to leave. Nevertheless it would have been a fool who underestimated Sir Hugh's ability to reach beyond the shores of England.

PREQUEL: 1765 – 1889

20

New Life

On the edge of Calais town Cleone and Albert took Suzanne to a circus where the three sat down at the ringside. Suzanne was thrilled and so absorbed by the spectacle that when the Ringmaster called a request for children who would like to ride the prancing horses Suzanne's face lit up. She was over the barrier and into the sawdust ring before anyone else. For a child of nine who had never been away from home or amongst other children, nor even ridden a horse, she had no fear, and not a thought that a child with an eye-patch would be noticed and recalled to mind. A lady took her hand and inexplicably, but quietly addressed her by her name.

'Come Suzanne, your horse awaits you.' The Ringmaster lifted each excited child up gently onto a horse's back tapping the animal on its rump to send it trotting round the ring. Round and round, Suzanne was enjoying herself so much she never noticed Cleone and Albert leave the big tent or that her mount turned quite smoothly out through the performer's tunnel and across the grass between the caravans, where Cleone and Albert were waiting alongside the lady from the ring who had used her name.

'How do you know my name?' Suzanne asked.

'I'm Helen, Sally's Aunt. Welcome to France. And this is my husband Paul. No he wasn't the real Ringmaster.'

Suzanne met the family, among them children of similar age to herself, sitting round the meal table. Here she learned a little more of Helen's story. Like Sally, she had fled from an unhappy life. Helen went to France where she married Paul Marceau who had rescued her from the water in mid-Channel. Rather than settling into village life, where she could possibly have been tracked down by her brother, Paul found work for them both with a travelling circus. Neither were performers. Paul's practical skills in carpentry and metalwork made him a valuable member of the troupe; keeping the properties well tended and safe for the travelling acrobats, high wire performers, jugglers and clowns. Since Helen arrived in France the pair had travelled with the circus people, they had produced three children of their own. Helen had become part of the group as controller of the company's finances, later being voted the one who fairly distributed their profits to all. 'As time goes by,' Helen said, 'you will learn how our group works. We hope you will be happy with us and find your part in our troop.'

'The Team winters just outside Paris,' Paul told Suzanne, we will be heading that way through the next few weeks. 'Now you must be very tired Suzanne so come along everybody to your beds. Ah, but wait a moment, Sally says that you have decided to change your name so before Cleone and Albert return to England, perhaps you would tell us what it's to be?'

Suzanne smiled. Her time had come.

'I am today, Carlotta McGuire' the little girl informed her new family.

Where she got the name from nobody knew and they didn't ask. It was entirely her choice. From that moment she was to be the owner of her new life.

Suzanne Lavender no longer existed.

21

Moving on

After leaving Lady Lavender's service Sally went home to her family where she stayed until she thought it safe to join Helen and the family at the Circus's winter home on the outskirts of Paris. Amy had kept Sally's share of the hidden gold safe, in fact she was surprised at just how much there was in the bundle. It gave her daughter independence. She was a wealthy young woman. Amy refused to have any of the money she wanted none of it and none of him, saying she had a husband and sons, she was perfectly happy. For now her family were her whole existence. Just to hear the clack of wood on wood and the grind of a saw coming from Tom and Will in the Carpenter's workshop; to picture her Mother and sisters working away in the fluff laden atmosphere weaving their cloth. At the far end of the yard a high pitched ting ting rang out as hammer hit metal on the anvil in the Blacksmith's forge, she was content and happy just to be at home and wait to hear how life for Sally, and her young charge unfolded, through Sally's letters home.

* * * *

When the troop at Circus Rouge first met Carlotta she was quite a small child a little girl with a patch over one eye just coming in to her tenth year. It was late autumn and the company was heading toward Paris and their last two venues before gathering at the winter sojourn on the outskirts of the city. By the time Sally joined them at the campsite it was all busy bustle sorting out properties for repairs and cleaning everything carefully ready for packing before each member was free to either return to their family homes or join the small troop performing for the season in the cafes and theatres in the city.

In her first letter to Amy, Sally told her Mother she found, 'A child transformed full of sparkling life and assurance. Oh Ma what a joy, she even had a new name.' While straight away Carlotta's comment was,

'Sally you're a lady now.' For she saw me, no longer dressed like a young peasant girl. As you know I was wearing a neat travelling suit carrying a valise, and like Tom told me, 'as a woman travelling alone; stand erect and be very collected.' But no outward differences prevented us from flying into each others' embrace, full of joy to be together again. Sally wrote that she had decided to stay with the Circus family until she got used to the language and living in France.

Her letter went on in a joyous whirlwind of words.

'Before I hardly had time to find the caravan where Carlotta slept or even put my valise away, I was swept up into their excitement of being in Paris. Only that morning a summons had come from a group of Ladies who wished to be entertained, "Lift our spirits." they commanded. Carlotta grabbed my arm, "Come on Sally you're coming too." Sally reported a carriage had been sent to take the troop into the city and as we rolled along the group, the six of us, discussed how to work. We would be Mummers make no sound. "Just mime along with us," they said, and described how, "I was given a full face mask a cone was placed on my head and I was to, hold onto any props thrown at me. I was in a whirl listening to all the excitement." Sally's words sent images of exotic costumes flung in well rehearsed, breathless organisation. As she commented, she had to learn their methods, on the hoof.

Sally explained that it was a dull cold winter day, the kind of day that kept a group of matron ladies in a closely draped elegant candlelit drawing room playing a silent game of cards, and with little else to occupy their minds except to complain about the sparse news they received of their husband's exploits. 'It is surprising what you overhear when you are a silent mime character,' Sally made particular note in her letter, 'I heard how these women came together in Paris for the winter months from their widely far flung estates where often they had few, or no other women of their own age or station in life, and apart from overseeing the farms and household business, were alone and left listening for the Post horn to bring news of their men folk's return. This group of women's husbands were Marshalls of the Republic, who were absent for many months serving the Emporer, gathering armies for his cause. Meanwhile the women were gathered at the apartment of the oldest member enjoying a gossip in each other's company. Their only exercise was sipping from their tall stemmed glasses of cordial, swaying and giggling growing evermore tipsy and sleepy as the hours passed.'

'Our troop entered the room behind two clowns, one sad the other cheeky causing modest titters.' Sally said she was glad she was able to watch from behind the mask. The two clowning had been summoned to entertain at this salon before so they knew just the kind of jokes to say; like whispering winds close to these elderly ladies ears, it wasn't long before gales of laughter filled the room so great that a maid had to bring pots from the cupboard for three elderly granddames to relieve themselves; at the instant they did so the clowns transformed themselves into a cows grazing the carpet without a care in the world. A barely controlled hand wave brought serving girls in with hot chocolat in deep saucer cups; as the drink was slurped Sally said she could see why the saucers were deep so to avoid hot liquid spilling over the swaying ladies.

Behind the anonymity of the mask Sally watched like a proud Mother as Carlotta flew silently into the room as if out of nowhere jerking the ladies onto wakefulness. The little figure stopped waited and when the fluttering surprise died down she sang a song of happy times when young love made hearts beat and sweet lips touched like butterflies. All breathing seemed to stop until one of the older Lady's exclaimed,

"What a dainty child so graceful and sweet, can I persuade the little girl to show what she is hiding behind the patch over her eye?" At first Carlotta showed reluctance but finally relented giving the tipsy old lady a private peep. The lady was so tickled she threw her head back giving out a raucous laugh saying,

"The child performed such a clever piece of magic she must be rewarded. Choose a gift," she crowed, flapping her scrawny hand suggesting, "something from the table."

"Your cup and saucer, if you please Madame it's far cleverer than my eye." The comment made the owner laugh even more. So much so the old lady pronounced that in her opinion such a clever choice made her afternoon. The blue and white china Trembleur was given to Carlotta with a ceremony of great aplomb and general amusement.

As the time went by Sally told of Carlotta's progress in training with the troop on the trapeze and how as her strength grew she became a central figure in their routine.

When Carlotta learned the juggling art so did Sally; when Carlotta learned to ride a horse so did Sally; but she drew the line saying that was enough for her when the fearless Carlotta stood up on the horse's back dancing turning somersaults and waving to the crowds of cheering onlookers. Every moment of each year was filled with performances punctuated by breaking down the tents, packing properties and moving on. Finally Sally decided it was time for her to move and go travelling with new found friends. Staying in Chateau and mountain Chalet; at Inns and city apartments, her wealth took her among the wealthy with ease. Her recently acquired skills among the shivering mystery of the circus people gave her a cache in the salons of those who felt their own lives were boring and mundane.

Sally assured Carlotta she was in a position to take care of herself, by telling her friend how on the last night, when her father Abel brought her home and so roughly, in his anger threw her in the door, a pouch had dropped from his saddle bag. Amy had seen it happen, watching where it fell in the stable yard and retrieving it later, but told no-one. The pouch had contained a large quantity of French gold. And of course nobody ever knew how wealthy Sally was. She never married. She remained her own woman, travelling gaining many friends and a wide circle of acquaintances in an unusual stratus of society. But we all need our special friends and Sally was Carlotta's lifelong friend.

22

Poise

At the age of twenty Carlotta was a young woman of great poise and attraction. In the intervening years she had made many City friends who called in to see her when she and the Company spent the winter rest months in Paris.

She became well known as the lady behind the stylish eye-patch. It was fashioned by the clever circus costumier in silk gauze allowing Carlotta to see clearly with both eyes. She could see you but you could not see what lay behind the patch.

In those years from age nine until 20 she had travelled in the circus with her French family revelling in the excitement on the high wire and trapeze. Her unusual gracefulness made her a sort after guest in the artistic winter salons of Paris. Like a ballerina she seemed hardly to touch the floor causing much admiring comment.

At fifteen Carlotta joined Helen and Paul's children to tour with a travelling troop going beyond the borders of France. They all wanted to experience life in other countries and learn other languages. Carlotta certainly achieved her ambition. It was noticed in prestigious gatherings she could soon speak fluently to anyone in their own tongue.

Not only did this graceful creature communicate with everybody she looked gorgeous. Her skin glistened like Mother of Pearl and her long raven black hair was thick and lustrous. That wasn't all. She smelled of delicate flowers. Carlotta washed her body and her hair and kept her clothes fresh laundered. Unusual for most people those days but she and Sally had started their lives living in an imposed solitary domain doing things their way, always practicing clean healthy bodily hygiene

As attractive as she was, Carlotta's friends, seeking to enjoy her company found that they were never fully allowed into her innermost feelings. Carlotta said herself, she was determined never to let anybody violate her being as her parents had once intended.

The realisation of the act they were planning had left her so deeply shocked. She knew that the barrier of reserve she held keeping friends just a little at bay must have made her quite hard for those well intentioned friends to get really close, especially when she was younger. Now in maturity she could empathise knowing others had their own problems. Nevertheless she remained somewhat abrasive if anyone ventured to come near her physically, until Philippe.

When he first set eyes on Carlotta, Philippe was in Paris on business and staying with friends who had persuaded him to accompany them to a musical evening at the great Opera singer Madam Ardemavner's Salon. Sitting well to the side of the drawing room Philippe was bored. Having seen enough of the darkly candelabra shadowed gold plasterwork and dramatic murals his gaze wandered over men and women in their elegant clothes. Through an atmosphere thick with heavy perfume he watched the signals of lust by men in over-powdered wigs who lolled, some leering at women with rouged encrusted creased skin who made lazy gestures of assignation with their fans held in heavily ringed fingers, some tipped with murky black nails. Central to the gathering their hostess stood tall and grand, her arms flung wide, acting out all emotion behind a voice whose volume rent the air on high diving octaves.

Philippe wasn't interested in this entertainment either and now could only think what an ear battering he was experiencing. Looking around at the upturned faces he smiled broadly to himself in amusement. Every countenance around him was becoming transfixed far more by the Diva's pair of impressive bosoms fighting to climb out of her bodice; the men obviously expectant, the women secretly squirming with bitchy glee behind the mock horror, except one, whose gaze appeared to be deferentially focused on the singer's face. More unusual was this young woman's lack of jewellery or heavy rouging on the pearly white profile and slender neck. A slight movement as she raised her hands in applause offered him a glimpse of long dark eyelashes. He was intrigued. Amid the standing noisome applause the glossy black head slowly but very deliberately turned and looked straight at him. How could she have known? The unexpected sight of just one deep brown eye surprised him as much as her apparent knowledge that he had been staring at her back view.

94

Her long steady look allowed him to see that her left eye was covered by a shallow black gauze cone outlined with tiny diamonds flashing in the candle light. Phillipe noticed other men's glances toward the Beauty were like invisible rays colliding across the room.

Catching hold of his friend's elbow, Philippe requested he be introduced to the 'Beauty in Black'. The man responded discretely leading Philippe through the crowd. Bowing graciously to the still seated young woman the friend asked in a modified voice, 'Mademoiselle may I have the honour to introduce the Count Philippe d'Ville?' With a smile and a nod of assent Carlotta modestly lowered her eyes.

'Count, this is Mademoiselle Carlotta McGuire.' As she slowly extended her un-gloved hand Carlotta claimed his eyes all the while he kissed the tips of her fingers. In her diary Carlotta wrote, '- - and so I met the only man I have ever loved.'

Sally's letter home told Amy she had been in Paris at a great Diva's Salon, 'Ah!' my Carlotta. She looked so beautiful.' Sally sounded like a long sigh as she recalled the whole scene of that evening. Even from where she had stood away in the shadows observing silently, Sally said she could feel the frisson between Carlotta and Phillipe.

Her dear little one, with the 'difference,' had gained a life, something at one stage Sally feared the little girl would never have.

PREQUEL: 1765 – 1889

23

Carlotta tells her diary

From that moment we drank each other in. Not to the full, not yet. My story is of sweet harmony and brutal cruelty.

I had no idea who or what he was. What I did know from those first moments was his uncanny understanding of MY feelings. No, this did not make me feel uncomfortable, far from it. I felt I had met the other half of myself. He was a darling in every aspect of our time together. But that is going ahead too fast. I did not know on that January evening when we first met, that Philippe had planned to return to his home the following day. We met everyday thereafter and one of the first things he told was that he was a Widower. As our friendship grew, my friends touched me with their joy for my visible happiness and their further, now amused, complaints of my neglect of them.

When my Circus family went back on the road in the spring their plan was to go north into the Russia's. Although I had been keen to experience the palaces and the people, I did not go with them. Instead I accepted an invitation from Philippe to visit his home. He had at no time pressed himself upon me. So with Sally to accompany me as chaperone and personal maid we travelled in his coach while he and one of his stewards rode horseback.

The journey was not too tedious for the coach wasn't overly sprung and the driver knew his horses and the road well. Over the years I have experienced riding in carts, carriages and caravans at a slower pace of course. Some were bone shaking causing me to alight and walk at my leisure or even hop up behind a rider. But that was when I was a child.

We travelled for two days. On the afternoon of the second day Philippe ordered our coach halted at the head of a long valley. The sun had well past its zenith. As he handed me down he told me we had been on his estate for the past three hours. Ushering Sally and me across the hillside we came upon a view so beautiful, pale gold in the early evening light. I remember gasping, for the sight clutched my heart.

One side of the wide sweeping valley was already in part shadow. At the far end stood a chateau, looking like a tiered wedding cake, on a shallow mound; something like the Manor house where I was born, but this was far more like a romantic dream its peachy pink walls glowed in the setting sun, a mirror image smiled up from the water of a surrounding lake.

No words passed between us for a while. Philippe motioned for our cloaks to be brought from the coach. As he lifted the garment around my shoulders he whispered, "You have no words?" I couldn't tell him exactly what I thought, for all I could think was, 'I've come home,' but that would have sounded very presumptuous as would the feeling I had that my whole body filled with a sensuous glow creating in its depth a perfect climax. So I simply said what I thought would please him,

'Such a beautiful sight it takes my breath away.'

Three great hounds – brindled grey – waited at the top of the steps to the side of the entrance, watching but keeping their distance.

As we ascended to the top of this flight of wide upsweeping piece of architecture a gentleman came from within and waited in the arching doorway. Philippe stopped, put his left arm across in front of me then turned to his three sentinels who, given their signal loped happily over to greet us showing their pleasure at his return.

"Zara, Ruben, Mario may I introduce Carlotta," As he said my name he withdrew his arm. The animals moved forward to acknowledge me but did not come within my reach. It was early days. Their loyalty was for their master who they were there to protect. Although the three became our shadow they always kept their distance. Not until this introduction was over did Philippe introduce me to the gentleman now stepping forward.

"Carlotta, this is my Major Domo, Armand. Armand this is Mademoiselle Carlotta McGuire and her friend Mademoiselle Sally Hartshorn."

"Enchanté Mademoiselles." he replied with a deep bow.

Philippe was like a small boy wanting to make me feel at home in his lovely chateau. The soft coral pink façade with its welcoming heart shaped arched entrance before the doorway opened into a grand reception hall, gave a surprisingly more severe masculine ambience than I expected, while the spacious ground floor rooms were very homely, after the grandeur the reception hall.

At first I had the feeling of being watched but there was not a soul in sight. Releasing Armand to his other duties Philippe wanted me to see every room unhindered by other people. Other people, I thought. What other people? Who? How many?

Set at the rear of the hall a wide central staircase rose up, parting at the first floor like the branches of a tree. Beckoning me to follow, Phillippe walked to the side of the wide central staircase. It seemed he was walking toward a blank wall. Not so, we passed into a long low warm comfortable ground floor sitting room its whole length ahead opening onto a deep galleried terrace that faced away down the opposite end of the valley we had first viewed from earlier that evening. This rear valley was not so elegant, more rural and soft I would say. Natural perhaps, un-landscaped, not needing to inspire like its front counterpart.

Our guest apartments were directly above the sitting room in a two storied part of the chateau having canopied verandas on the first floor to view the terrace below that opened out into a courtyard surrounded by gardens and a high wall. Philippe told us this was all part of his private domain.

On this visit I wasn't' shown any further but looking back from the far side of the walled garden I could see why my first impression of the chateau was of a tiered cake. Rising above the private apartments and stepped back a third storey of rooms with a heavily foliaged garden on the roof, behind and above one could just see a further layer of windows. Set to the side in the lake and attached to the main buildings by a short causeway stood a majestic round tower rising five storeys with stables and courtyards segmented around the base.

We spent a luxurious week. Mine and Sally's bedrooms each had their own bath chambers. It was very feminine, though maybe a touch old fashioned in their decor, but beautifully scented fresh blooms were brought in from the gardens every morning. We walked, danced, played cards and dined well. My times in private with Philippe were idyllic. I wished it could last forever.

You know, I was very naughty. On one or two nights I scaled the veranda, the gardens and the high walls. It was no problem for me. My curiosity had been fed over the past five years. Wherever the circus had stopped I visited all the secluded places in the towns and villages, overhearing much that I should not have known.

A black body suit gives one access to places where you are never seen because your presence is not expected.

I did see there was yet a further two courtyards either side of the round building. They looked strangely empty although one could have been used for strenuous ball games. I found the round building most curious. It only had narrow apertures at intervals but I could see light through giving me to believe the light inside came centrally from the moon above.

Taking note of soft light and movement inside the windows of the main building I kept well away not wanting to be caught in any unexpected encounter that might embarrass my host.

Over the course of the week I learned Philippe was twenty five years my senior. I was surprised as his looks and athletic body made him appear ten years younger. His wife had died not long after the birth of their twin sons, who were now in their twenty-first year and recently inherited their mother's properties abroad.

So, he had been a widower for a little over twenty years and was a very wealthy landowner.

At the end of my stay Philippe asked me, with a little twinkle in his eye if I had liked everything I had seen, with the emphasis on the 'everything.'

'You haven't shown me everything. I haven't seen your tower.'

'But you have.'

'Not the rooms inside.'

'No those we must leave for another occasion.'

'I can tell you Philippe that this week has been the happiest of my life so far.'

'Darling I accept that truth with deep humility. I do not think you have ever revealed such inner thoughts before. I can't offer you my youth Carlotta but I can give you security and my love.'

I was so …. I could not readily put into words the value of his maturity and care for my happiness and well being, riches beyond riches.

'Would you consent to be my wife?'

'Philippe you have never asked to see behind my eye-patch.'

'No my dear, that would not be necessary.'

I removed the covering over my eye. I had to it would have been unfair to agree to become his wife without him knowing everything about me. The unaccustomed bright light forced me to shade my eye, which made him think I was flinching from his gaze but we soon overcame that misconception. At first his expression showed anger that changed to sorrow.

'My poor girl', he said with such sadness, 'is this what your mother called an aberration?' But then he laughed taking me in his arms and kissing me lovingly, 'My darling it's beautiful. Nobody in their right mind would want to eradicate such a magnificent … difference.' I replaced the patch, stunned at his reaction.

'You do not need to do that for me. But I see you are so used to keeping the unusual a secret. Why not, let's leave it a lovely mystery!'

I came to Philippe's life with experiences far beyond most women of my times let alone my age. I was the same age his first wife was when she lost her life and when he felt his had ended. I had kept my virginity intact that was never for any man's passing fancy.

'Philippe, I give you all the love I have', I replied, 'it would be an honour and a joy to be your wife.'

To some my choice appeared sudden and rushed. To Sally, who had witnessed our love grow knew it was all perfectly natural. My French family and my friends gave us their blessing. Who else was there to tell?

PREQUEL: 1765 – 1889

24

Honey years

I can only tell my diary the truth. You won't want to read my diary in future years only to learn the story of an idyllic life. No, people want to find out the exciting revelations, the strange and the unusual.

Be patient.

Two months later I became the Countess Carlotta d'Ville McGuire at a private ceremony with Sally and just our household family in attendance. Philippe made me his equal. A true partnership then was unusual but we were an unusual couple.

We had each travelled widely in France to Vienna and to Prague, Philippe into the Iberian Peninsula and across in England. We each spoke a wide variety of languages.

Our moon of honey love was exhilarating free and full of gentle tenderness. Spring burst into summer the air was sparkling with colours, perfumed from the flowers and fruits in the fields and hedgerows. We walked hand in hand for miles, sometimes stopping at the farms to greet Philippe's tenants. They weren't just tenants they were his family. I was introduced by my first name and he gave me theirs. He asked after members of their wider family and they asked after his sons and mother. He knew everyone and listened carefully. I know for a fact his estate steward visited and attended to their requests, very soon thereafter. And even though it was our honeymoon Philippe received his reports. I didn't leave any homestead without a small gift of flowers or maybe a tiny quail's egg.

Other days we rode out further afield, Philippe's hounds alongside. My husband had given me my own horse, a Palomino. She was beautiful, my friend and protector.

Late of an evening we swam, as the moon climbed high above the crystal clear lake. Making love in the water swirling and diving in an orgasmic rhythm. Chasing and rolling in the long grass like children at play. This experience was pure, explosive addictive even, seeming never ending.

Here was freedom unbounded; release into the joy of life once denied to me by my English parents, wiping my childhood days into oblivion.

Late on a bright morning after a long ride, we arrived at a high rocky outcrop. Philippe dismounted and without looking back ran forward to the rock face and started to climb Zara, Ruben and Mario sat waiting in a group near our horses. Wearing culottes I was able to catch up scaling the surface in my own manner. After a long steep ascent we arrived at the top together. Not once had he put out a hand to help me. Sitting side by side on the summit our legs hanging over the edge we viewed the valley beyond.

'Now you know why I quite naturally pronounced you my equal Carlotta. You never took me at face value nor I; you. Like fighters in life we each watched the other before making our decisions.'

He knew I had surveyed his home those nights. By now he was acquainted with my curious skills. I could climb and swing my body between anything, anywhere.

I just smiled. We needed no more words.

* * * *

My apartments in our private quarters contained everything for my comfort. I had the decoration kept light and airy in soft colours of pale turquoise blue and creamy yellow to reflect the southern sky. The sun shone gently all day onto the house. A colonnaded walkway sheltered the ground floor rooms and canopies shading the widows above the first floor. Below my bedroom windows a courtyard garden spread in a semicircle in front of the colonnaded walk. Shrubs and flowering trees gloriously muddled with vines and climbing plants; its vista was a charmingly romantic space filled with the sweetest smelling plants and trees full of places to settle whatever the time of the year. My husband told me I could root it all out if I had a mind. But no, I could feel the love that had gone into its original planting; even the romance that flourished among the foliage. So my re-planning went into pruning to let in more light and encourage strong healthier growth.

* * * *

Before we could start our journey to visit Philippe's family, his mother, Rhoda, arrived unannounced late one evening. Philippe was not at all surprised. Although in her late eighties Rhoda was still a formidably strong willed outgoing character. Tall like her son, elegant and beautifully dressed. Again, like her son she looked much younger than her actual years. Her steward had ridden ahead, but only one hour ahead, to warn the household to prepare her apartment.

Gerard, our house steward was not put out. He always kept the rooms in readiness. He knew his Master's mother of old.

My husband told me how in her usual way she came sweeping in calling,

'Philippe, where is she?'

The Dowager Countess Rhoda d'Ville had to be disappointed, 'What do you mean she's staying with friends, without her husband?'

When the old Countess had been settled with a hot chocolat in her sitting room she conversed more calmly.

'Maman, my new young wife has a life of her own, as do I.' Philippe told her.

'Nonsense, Philippe. How can such a young married woman have a 'life of her own' as you call it?'

'You do Maman.'

'Phaw, I am old and alone I run my own establishment, enough of this, tell me about her.'

'What do you want to know?'

'Everything of course, you omitted to come to ask my advice. I know nothing of this girl. Where does she come from?

'She is what would be known as a Cosmopolitan.'

'Good heavens man that tells me nothing.'

'What am I? Born in France, yes, but I know many countries, speak their languages. Carlotta is like me.'

'That is silly. You are a Frenchman, Philippe.'

'Then we will say Carlotta is an Englishwoman, the land where those of many countries make their home.'

'I can believe that. The English are a mish-mash of humanity.' His Mother chortled.

'Oh they wouldn't like to hear that Maman' Philippe replied amused at her humour.

'I hear she is a great beauty but somewhat unusual?'

'You hear well Maman. What else do you hear?'

'Don't play with me my son. I want to know how it is with you.'

'My darling, I am the happiest, luckiest man in the world. Carlotta is sweet and loving. She is an athlete.'

'A what?'

'An athlete.'

'She's surely a woman. What kind of athlete if you please?'

'I mean she rides well, dances with grace, and plays stringed instruments with sensitivity. She is assured in the company of others from many races.'

'And you've left her alone. If she is so independent what makes you think she won't run away? You're not a young man.' Philippe laughed. 'Phshaw!' his mother exclaimed, 'do not laugh Philippe, I say only the truth.'

'Mother, we are equals. She has had a full life, even in only twenty years.'

'Are you planning to tell her all you do here?'

'Most. Not all. Not yet.'

'What if she finds out before you can tell her yourself my son?'

'Carlotta has more experience of human kind at twenty than I had at that age. She's a woman of the world. I have shown her much of my Business most of it is quite obvious. Before I can bring her fully into its depth I do have other areas in our lives together that I want to prepare.'

'You mean offspring I imagine.'

'Yes that too Maman.'

'Well, I can hardly wait to meet this 'love of your life'.'

'Now you are making fun of me' Philippe commented, 'but I deserved that.' He smiled with indulgence.

'Leave me now, I must rest. I'm not a young woman anymore, gallivanting across the country!' The Dowager Countess Rhoda d'Ville slept for 48 hours.

Helen and Paul were only a few miles away with Circus Rouge when we were at the end of our Months of Honey love, so I took Philippe to meet them both and their two daughters, Amy and Elsa, their son Vincent was away with a travelling group at the time. Paul and Philippe had much to talk over. It was a surprise me to learn that the two men had done business in the past. It was such a delight being with Helen for the while and we had so much to catch up on. I learned Sally was on a journey to Florence with a group of women friends, and in Amy's last letter she told how her three young boys were all working with their father Tom, since he had inherited the Carpentry shop after the death of his father, Will Hartshorn.

Philippe needed to return home for his business affairs so I stayed two more days to travel with the troupe to their next venue which brought them even nearer my new home.

This was to be Helen and Paul's final year with circus Le Rouge. They told me of their plans to farm on land they had acquired adjacent to Helen's sister Elsa. Sally had also put some funds into the farm to give herself her permanent home for the times when she resting from her travels. All the members of my adopted family would not be so far away after all.

On my return home I was told of the Dowager's presence but she was still resting, so that gave me time to freshen up for my presentation.

I met with her approval.

We walked together in the gardens and talked under awnings in the autumn warmth. Sipping cool drinks and laughing at women's woes I wished I'd had a mother like Rhoda. We became firm friends, I at twenty, she at eighty-eight. After only a week she announced, 'Now I am leaving you. Nobody wants their old mother about when they are newly married.'

Before she left Rhoda said to me. 'Thank you for making my son happy again my dear. I love you all the more for that.'

Almost ninety years old but determined to keep her dignity and her independence she climbed unaided up into her carriage. I'm sure she knew there were arms and hands ready to steady her but her servants were careful not to make any show of their mistress's physical fallibility.

Her maid tucked the travelling rugs snugly round the old legs and I noticed Rhoda patted the young woman's hand in thanks. For all her apparent bossiness to her son she was a sweet tempered lady who was concerned like any mother for her child. Age does not change relationship of love.

* * * *

The reception rooms on the ground floor and the first floor at the front of chateau were used for Philippe's clients. There was no ostentatious decoration no chandeliers rather low lighting was set beside each chair by double candle light. There were no mirrors.

Men came to relax, to play cards to read and smoke. They played billiards and table games; like Majong; dined well in private dining rooms and stayed in the suites of single chambers on the floors above.

The courtyards beyond, away from our private area, served for ball games, wrestling and eastern style combat. Stables provided horses for riding and other competitive pursuits.

Philippe introduced me into all the lower saloons so that his wife was known and would be the only woman seen near the men's domain.

I was taken through the passages where I could see and not be seen for my presence was not wanted within their relaxing areas. I learned the intimate details of the business and its membership which had been part of his family for three generations.

My introduction to one member on this first occasion seemed more solemn. Hands were shaken when normally, I would, as a woman, have held my hand out to be brushed with a courtly kiss. This was altogether different, this was professional..

Later Philippe explained this man was a politician and would become very influential. 'I will always make sure these men know who you are Carlotta. Take note, they are the men who could impact on all our lives in the future.'

All the staff knew me of course and I made sure I was familiar with all their faces. But I only had regular contact with Armand and our house steward Gerard, and naturally my own maid, Lucy.

About the great tower Philippe told me little only that it was set aside for astronomers, further activities he would show me later. I had so much of interest in our own apartments that I had no time for the men or the star watchers. I was a wife. Life was peaceful and, yes, fun too.

* * * *

After Maria's demise Philippe was very reluctant to allow me to go through childbirth, he didn't want me to suffer and lose my life like his dear sweet Maria. Or even lose his own 'second wonderful chance,' as he put it.

The evening before we married Philippe gave me a delicately etched gold locket. Lifting the chain over my head, to nestle the locket down between my breasts he told me, 'I leave this in your charge. Use it tomorrow night my darling please. Opening the jewel I found a black silk pouch and all neatly folded inside was a condom made of gossamer thin pigskin intestine, the end closed with a fine silk thread.

Of course eventually the inevitable happened anyway. We were both thrilled at the prospect for he really hadn't wanted to deprive me of the joy of having my own child.

Two years after we married our little daughter, Isabella, was born. Philippe was ecstatic. He could have been her grandfather for most men his age were great-grandfathers by then. Age made him an indulgent and patient father. We were so pleased that Isabella had come soon enough for Rhoda to see her.

Joy of joys, Philippe's sons came from the Indies to see their grandmother and their new sister just a month before Rhoda passed away in her ninety first year.

Robert and Dominick were not identical twins. I'm told one looked just like his mother whilst the other could have been Philippe facially, but only came up to his father's shoulder. He was

short and broad. Both young men had Philippe's kind manners and
gentle character. I liked them very much.

Caring for our baby was such a happy experience for me. She
had a nursemaid who gave me guidance but I was her mother and
I breastfed her myself. After the total indifference I experienced
from my own mother, I was determined to give my baby all the
maternal love I was deprived. It may not have been fashionable for
a woman of my station to breast feed. I was not interested in what
was fashionable or otherwise. I had only ever seen my mother very
briefly and then after we had heard her call from the anteroom – 'Is
the child covered?'

Sally and I had to make very sure no part of my eye was visible.
Once my mother feigned being sick and bolted for the door. I don't
remember her ever touching me. I used to feel so rejected but Sally,
bless her put my mind into a sensible channel. 'Don't think of her as
your mother, it will only make you sad. Never allow them to pour
that emotion onto you. It is their self imposed disappointment, not
yours.' she counselled.

She was right. I had Sally. She was my support at all times and
the only one worth my love. She always made me feel strong and
loved.

My father never came to see me, but I saw him. Oh yes. I was
an athlete, if you want to call it that, long before I experienced the
circus training.

The house at Moat Mount was ancient, with additions over
the many years, its roof spaces had openings between all parts of
the building. I knew the roof and wall cavities like the back of
my hand – and of course I was only small so I could penetrate
where no man had access since it was built. There were many areas
where I could look down upon the people below. Not just in the
upper rooms. Two of the ground floor rooms were great halls, one
a chapel, but other downstairs apartments had secret passages by
then unused, probably never known by my parent's generation.
There were times when I listened and watched my father conducting
secret negotiations with leading Politicians. He had no notion of my
presence nor even would he have recognised me excepting that my
eye patch gave me away.

* * * *

Once Isabella was weaned Philippe and I were able to spend a few days in Paris where we attended the opera, the theatre and after at Salons where we met the artistes. Philippe had never cared much for opera but as I wanted to accept the invitations, he indulged me and of course it was safer for me to travel with my husband. On two occasions we visited the opera in Venice moving on to stay a while in Florence and Sienna.

It was when we went across to England, to the opening of the Theatre Royal in Brighton in 1807, I once again saw my father.

On this occasion both Philippe and I were guests of George, the Prince Regent, who had once or twice, in his youth, stayed here at the chateau. Philippe knew of George's womanising so was glad to be protector to me and Sally, who was in our party, she being a long time friend of Maria Fitzherbert. They had met in France when I was a child in the Circus. Those were the days Sally enjoyed her freedom to travel and study.

George's theatre was very plain, almost austere compared with those in Paris and Venice but the audience was equally loud although their words more subdued.

Many in the audience were on their feet giving the performance a standing ovation, "Capital and Charming." The response was fulsome while I wasn't the only one looking around the auditorium at the gathering; I noticed a man in a box opposite looking straight at us through a glass. I'll have no truck with people who stare so I nodded and smiled. He gave himself away immediately by suddenly lowering the glasses. I had caught him out. To him, I would have appeared quite brazen – then he would have learned I was from France, so what else could he expect!

I knew it was him. He was by then a very elderly man but no mistaking the one thing that remained in my memory of that formal black satin knot he always wore at his throat. My mother wasn't present. I doubt she would have recognised me. I was rather sad for her not him though, I couldn't forgive him.

* * * *

Our Isabella showed her fullest love for us both. She was growing into a beautiful young woman. Not overly keen to join society. They were far too fuddy-duddy for her liking, too encumbered by ritual. Instead she practiced painting the plants in our gardens, and the wider landscapes around.

We travelled with her to Switzerland where she made paintings of the alpine plants whilst we walked the mountains, leaving our daughter attended by a male guard and her personal servants.

This was my first visit to the Alps. I found these new surroundings alive with fascinating folk traditions. The people in their National dress seemed to meld into the landscape. The air gently wafted with clear sharp aromas. It was on these walks in the mountains that Philippe began to tell me how to carry on his business after him and to manage the future for our Daughter's inheritance.

He must have had some presentiment.

The chateau held secrets only to be passed to family. Like Philippe the servants had also inherited their positions. If Philippe was no longer with us I had to master the knowledge to pass it on to the boys and our daughter when she reached twenty-five.

On our return home we started by traversing the main building and all that lay within its intricate network of secret passages. In the first year of our marriage my husband had shown me the entry points into the main rooms by staff whilst on their service duties, were often via parts that appeared to be blank endings camouflaging slewed curves through which a body, carrying slim tiers of trays, could sidle to gain entrance to stairways up or down. To begin with it was bewildering the number of small secluded apertures to allow viewing and listening.

In one of the longer spaces below ground I was surprised to see a group of members playing out a war game on great landscaped table with painted lead soldiers. By the unguarded conversation we heard, this sounded more than a game. Above, the first floor rooms were less for sleeping than for personal games and decorated to suite the service required. I recognised some of the contraptions and comforts

I had stumbled upon when, as a child, I had strayed into the wrong caravan or peeped into rooms in houses where our troop had been hired to entertain.

'But Philippe, you said no other woman would ever be allowed in here.'

'So I did, and you are correct. No lady. These men and women are supplied when needed and returned after their service is completed.'

'You included men?'

'Yes, some of our members are bi-model for choice. All is catered for.'

Going on in some detail Philippe showed me the item that gave entry to the club. He explained how to recognise a genuine piece from an imitation at a brief glance. I, as a woman had to avoid showing doubt in a man, especially if his talisman turned out to be genuine.

As the occasion would have it that day, we were passing through one of the passages, when Armand silently appeared as if out of a blank wall and beckoned to my husband. Philippe turned telling me to follow closely.

'Now wait here and observe' he ordered. I found myself directed to look through a glass eyepiece giving clear view down into the Reception Hall and saw Philippe, followed a pace behind by Armand, enter the hall and walk across to a gentleman who was standing just inside the entrance, still holding his hat and gloves. The visitor immediately extended a hand to Philippe. Taking the proffered hand my husband seemed to hold it longer than was usual. The visitor in turn looked somewhat taken aback. Then oddly there was a chinking sound as a distorted gold band hit the marble floor followed by dusty debris of small pieces of stone. An astonished look spread across the visitor's face whilst a thin smile crossed Philippe's lips as he said,

'Goodbye Monsieur.' His face suffused with anger the visitor attempted to speak but before he could do so Armand was firmly ushering him out.

I could see through to the entrance yard that the visitor's coach had been retained at the bottom of the steps by one of our staff.

As the coach drove away down the long drive my husband came back to the passage. Standing beside me he said, 'Do you spy two figures on horseback there, look, over in the tree line. They will follow. We want to know where he goes.'

'Philippe, how did you know?'

'We know who is invited to become a member. This man was not.'

'But how did you crush that ring in your hand?'

'I palmed the ring it did not fit him for it was stolen. Your friends in the circus are not the only conjurors, my love.' The ring lay in his hand, intact.

'But – ?' I questioned, Philippe held up his other hand to allay my question. In a small leather drawstring pouch I was shown the apparent debris of the ring that only members can wear.

The gold banded ring of membership held a hard stone in varying shades of pale green carved with the head of Venus with the legend that a genuine piece could not be shattered. This is why the ring would have to be stolen for the bogus visitor to be in possession of the real thing. What wasn't realised was that each numbered ring is made to order and carefully documented. The members entering this chateau need total secrecy. This was not only a place of pleasure and relaxation but of secrets and destinies ... destinies? So I thought I knew the whole source of the d'Ville's family wealth creation.

Unfortunately my husband's time ran out before he explained the final reason for all the secrecy.

* * * *

Philippe and I had almost twenty happy years together. For me it was all too short. I had lost the love of my life.

Although he was seventy, my husband looked a healthy fit man, very athletic. I later discovered this very lifestyle had taken his strength suddenly, after his regular vigorous exercise routine that he undertook with a group of, what I had thought were just friends.

Armand sent my maid to me just after midnight. Philippe had been taken to his rooms from the exercise yard.

'The Master collapsed during the training session Madame.' I could see Armand had tears in his eyes. Philippe's life had gone.

I felt a cold hand turn my centre core to ice. I couldn't move, my face my hands, I felt paralysed by shock. Finally all I could do was drop to my knees beside the bed and rest my head on the pillow beside my dead husband. Armand stood at the foot of the bed and Philippe's closest group of staff, ten men, stood heads bowed by the door.

It must have been nearly half an hour before I or any of us moved again.

I knew that my time of greatest responsibility had come. Over the years Philippe had prepared me well.

Although I felt my heart broken I had no time to grieve. This was all part of Philippe's plan to put me in complete charge of the chateau; the membership and the estates. It would fill my time to the full. Even before my husband's body was moved and laid to rest, Armand handed me the keys and two letters. I shook hands making direct eye contact with each one of the ten. They bowed heads, then followed Armand to their immediate duties.

Back in the solitude of my bedchamber I found my instructions. One letter was to be opened first and the second to be read at noonday. In the first Philippe reiterated his instructions he had verbally given me, when he had so recently spoken of our daughter's inheritance. Armand would show me every further aspect of the business and be my trusted guide.

- *'Establish firm control from the very start', the letter told me, 'before my demise is known further than my ten men and yourself.'*
- *'Let nobody gain the upper hand' my husband's written words warned. 'I know your strength of character will prevail. Especially at a time of crisis.'*
- *'Keep a sharp awareness of the wider political situation.'*

The envelope also contained the mechanical lock codes to many more entrances in places I had not yet been made acquainted. These I had to memorise.

My first thoughts were for our daughter Isabella who sadly was away visiting her half brothers on their West Indian estates. She had grown as adventurous as her mother had been, so Philippe could hardly deny his daughter her wish to travel and have experiences. She was keen to paint the plants on the tropical islands so we had made sure she was well cared for travelling in known company with her servants.

It would be many months before my letters could reach her and Philippe's twin sons with the news of their Father's death. Concentrate on the immediate and practical came first. I therefore put the letters of these events away until later.

* * * *

Before dawn came Armand accompanied me through the lower reception rooms then up into the first floor where Philippe had already given me that brief viewing. Some rooms were currently occupied, those that were not, where the doors were ajar I entered to inspect.

'Leave these doors open Armand. It's business as usual.'

The rooms on the second floor were for sleeping alone and somewhat like small cells. They could be viewed from the secret passages so I chose to check them and sign off, clear. The courtyards, of which there were four, were unused at that hour and Armand assured me were in proper preparation. For what, I was to learn later?

Indicating the keys to the tower we entered the ground floor. Here I began to feel a little excited as well as apprehensive. Most of this area would, even after twenty years, be new to me.

As we ascended the stairs I saw we were encased in the wall around a large open space. At the level of where a roof would have been were alcoves for the purpose of viewing the stars. In each alcove was a telescope set above a seat, of, I was told, the latest design. The whole apparatus swivelled 180°, the huge thickness of the walls being a firm foundation for viewing the heavens on an ever moving earth.

Satisfied, I retreated to my apartments for breakfast and to allow Armand his time for prayer and food.

The business records in a locked cabinet had been delivered to my sitting room. Without delay I proceeded to scan these books whilst taking refreshment.

During my years of training with the circus Helen had shown me how to keep records and control finances.

'If you know what should be in the records you will see what's missing, what shouldn't be there, and the simply unusual.' She told me. These records revealed a great many more secrets under the surface. The wealth accumulated at the chateau was showing a value greater than the activities I already knew of could yield or even require.

When Armand returned to my apartment it was full light.

'Now we will go where the rest of these keys will take us Armand. I would like to be shown where the story in these record books takes place.'

With his usual slight bow Armand led me back to the tower entering this time from a door in a lower courtyard. No other servants accompanied us.

I found myself in a spacious elegant entrance hall opposite the main door. Taking a look behind me there was no sign of the door that I had come through. Apart from the full length windows either side of the main doors, the walls around were painted from ceiling to floor with displays of woodland scenes and distant views of rivers and mountains. I felt as if I were truly out in the open. A grand arch fronted a tunnel into a seated auditorium but Armand steered me away to where he lifted the edge of a tapestry revealing a small doorway within a cleverly carved stone crinkle wall. Preceding me he seemed to disappear into the stones.

'The heavy ornate key is for this lock.' Armand told me.

He followed me into a galleried balcony where I could look down into a sandy arena deep beneath the round tower.

'You are presently on the upper gallery that runs round the private seated area beside the arena Mistress. Above this is a larger seating area and salons for refreshment. A second private gallery runs round the tower similar to this one, with secret one way windows as you see here.'

Every two metres a small niche over the seating had an aperture allowing a wide view on the seating below.

'This ground floor area is separately entranced on the other side of the tower, where coaches await their owners away from view and use another driveway.'

We walked through the upper area and salons, some laid with tables for dining, others for resting and cleansing.

The passage above ran round the lower edge of the high vaulted ceiling. Away above this vaulted ceiling the tower walls housed all the alcoves for telescopes. Although the many candle sconces were not in use, the area below the vaulted roof was full of light.

'A voice on the opposite side of the auditorium, in this encircling passage, can be heard as if the speaker is talking in your ear' Armand explained.

Through further passages and hidden doorways we arrived down at the arena where low archways gave me entrance into the sandy circle. I walked out into its centre, which I estimated was 4 metres across, and looked up. So that's why the arena was so full of light. The vaulting high above had pierced lattice pattern stonework letting in the light from the sky.

Looking back around the circle of arches it was now evident that this was a large cage at the base of a funnel.

The lower viewing area slightly stepped back under the galleried balcony and therefore unseen from above and in shadow to those looking across the space.

Questions filled my mind but for the moment I kept them to myself.

Following Armand, who had waited outside the cage, we entered a changing room where he ushered me to a comfortable armchair and requested to also be seated. I nodded my approval and awaited explanations.

'This chamber is where the Emperor's directives are carried out under strict scrutiny and where his guests pay to watch the spectacle.'

'Directives! What kind of spectacle Armand, when?' He only answered my third question.

'On moonless nights Mistress.'

'Sounds very mysterious?' I almost laughed. But of course this finally answered the question I never fully understood during our years together. Philippe had taken to his own apartments for four days almost every month.

At first I had thought it was coinciding with my own monthly cycle but often it did not. I knew he wasn't far away in the exercise yards maybe, but never what he was actually doing. During those times I had also noticed there were fewer male servants in evidence.

'If I am right, tonight there is a waning moon?'

'You are correct Mistress.'

'Then I shall attend the spectacle, as you call it myself.'

'Thank you. Please be ready at eleven.'

It was by now noonday so I retired to my sitting room. The midday sun was hot outside and the air hardly moved. So much had passed since that tap on my bedroom door and the awful sight of my darling husband lifeless. The second letter written in his hand lay on the table beside my chair.

> *"My darling Carlotta, the night has come when you will finally be witness to the service our family has undertaken during the Emperor's reign. The experience may take all your powers of endurance. I apologise I have not been able to make you aware of this during my lifetime. It was for both our good.*
>
> *Armand, as ever, will be your guide.*
>
> *Neither his family nor our colleagues' families know the truth of their service.*
>
> *Now it falls to you to take the reins.*
>
> *The apparel for your new role you will find laid out in readiness for tonight and future events, night or day.*
>
> *Your Philippe."*

Wearing a full face mask and cloaked in matt black, I followed Armand through the passages to the tower. As we traversed to the highest level I noticed other figures similarly clad moving silently within the passages.

'They are our staff Mistress. This eye movement will prove each ones' legitimacy within these passages. And they can come and go amongst the gathering without being seen and never known. My master must have brought to your attention that ten male staff wear a ring similar to his own, the one you now wear.' I nodded in agreement.

'You see through here to this courtyard.' I did so. 'Carriages come to leave their occupants who enter the public door, then move off along the left hand colonnade to water their horses and wait. Those who wish their presence to remain anonymous, use a separate driveway and entrance, are also masked and cloaked and come in unmarked carriages.'

Philippe had told me the building had been originally designed for a religious sect more than a century ago. The layout allowed for high officials to keep their anonymity.

The figures entering the public door walking through onto the balcony level were dressed as if for a carnival. I could see those people meeting in the entrance hall and through in the salons at the rear of the seating. They preened themselves in their ostentatious, outrageous costumes showing off to the crowd around them.

Eager to know more about the occupants of the two tiers below I leaned forward into one of the niches.

The seats on the lowest level directly around the arena were quiet and dark. Ghostly figures moved between groups shaking hands, their cloaks swinging like great winged birds of prey. Some sat perfectly still. Leaning to the right I could hear the murmured conversations quite clearly coming from this dark peopled area. Leaning to the left the sound from the upper gallery was almost riotous, full of shrill laughter and expectation. The sights were even more extreme. A woman bare breasted in the old Court mode made her entrance, stood stock still, her haughty look demanding attention. I thought I could see a man bending down beside her until she gave a sharp tug on a leather leash bringing round the great head of a masked hound standing at her shoulder level. As she paraded into one of the salons I noticed the animal was clothed in dark breeches. Both men and women wore highly coloured garments rich in gold thread flouting their wealth. Some of the men had elaborately full shouldered jackets with tights exposing their naked buttocks and highly decorated penis pouches.

'Is this where the high income is derived, Armand?'

'Yes, Mistress those selling their opportunities pay very high premiums.'

I could see more women bare breasted in overly dramatic ways. One in particular caught my attention. I had seen her before somewhere, then, as her activity revealed her business I remembered how in my first winter sojourn with the Circus outside Paris a group of young women were being trained to retrieve coinage gifts from table tops and seated men's knees. Here was one of those very pupils now in her full bloom selling favours amongst her bare breasts while straddling the tables and men's knees collecting the gold coins in her vagina.

'She is known as "La Vagin."' Armand's quiet voice had noted the scene I was watching. I did not reply. It was quite sufficient my prior knowledge remained my own.

'Those who view pay more besides a membership fee. If they bring guests the price is according to their status and the number of actions staged at each event.'

The figures in the accounts were becoming clearer to me now. I let Armand explain further whilst I watched the mounting tensions below.

'The dark audience close to the arena edge are the highest returners and want it kept exclusively so.'

As my steward spoke I moved from niche into niche to find a clear view of all the levels of company. He followed discretely unfolding the story.

A shout pierced the noise. Voices below were quelled. Faces turned, raised and tried to focus in the direction of the sound but it was actually directionless. Failing the offer of an early spectacle the loud company reverted to their own crowd for amusement.

Armand was leaning back against the outer wall listening to the report of what had occurred.

'No fear mistress' Armand's voice remained low. Figures had moved forward along the passage, now retreated into the shadows again.

'Somebody has penetrated the inner sanctum detonating a warning shot.

I hear the all clear sign. He didn't get far. The stranger will not remember his unwarranted escapade when he returns to conscious state in a Paris back street.'

The lights grew brighter over the arena, the sounds of voices and laughter ceased and as the rustle of cloaks and full skirts found their seats the light abruptly died over the audience.

'Each lamp has its host Mistress' Armand had noted my surprise at the synchronised dousing of the lights. Two men emerged from the cage gated arches on opposite sides of the arena, proceeding directly to the centre where they bowed, each head lightly touching the other. I watched as the pair, dressed only in white breeches, wrestled in an almost balletic manner only lasting a few minutes before they halted at three chimes of a bell and backed away without taking their eyes off each other. When the bell sounded again the men moved in towards the centre crouching. The tussle became heated. The bell chimed twice. Nobody moved. The audience remained silent.

As the bell sounded for a third time the figures moved back four paces then with sudden lunges threw themselves at each other with shattering force. Locked together under the lights a low murmuring rhythm issued from sections of the upper balcony.

With a violently sudden movement one of the men lifted his opponent high above his head and brought him to the floor sitting himself on the man's almost deflated chest, but only for a moment. The bout was over. Clapping and a few calls followed the pair out of the arena.

The ground was swiftly brushed; the stewards leaving only just in time before the second pair, this time two women, ran into the circle of light. I thought at first they were about to juggle as they each flung away their skirts caught by the stewards behind them. At the sight of almost naked women the catcalls came like animal voices.

This was altogether a screeching drama of hair pulling scratching, pinching and bloodletting. Kicking and – horror – bone cracking. The audience were aroused to an ever greater fury of calls and arm flailing.

'The two women are the first of the prisoners Mistress.' There was certainly more to this event than pretty wrestling.

One of the women didn't rise. The other raised her arms and beat her fists up high in victory. Cheers roared as she swung to fro and round to receive the adulation. The prone figure leaped without a sound like an animal onto its prey, grabbing the unsuspecting ex-victor's hair. Hushed in shock the audience had given no sign to the standing figure. Her head wrenched from behind she was flung to the floor breaking her neck with a splintering crack.

A scream of victory rippled through the onlookers as the living woman snatched her skirts from the steward and walked away.

'That one gained her freedom Mistress. Prisoners can partake in a lottery to fight for their freedom between every full moon.'

After each bout I noticed those on the balcony standing on their seats each with a different numbered white plaque raised high.

A lone figure came to the centre of the arena looked around and pointed a wand at a number.

'What are they doing Armand?'

'Bidding for the corpse Mistress some are relatives if they are lucky. Others just want the corpse for other uses' he answered then carried on, 'the corpses are delivered to the owner's carriage to await their final fate.'

'What other uses?' I felt the horror rising in my throat. Immediately I realised I had shown my womanly concern. Although this was to Armand I quickly resolved to hide my emotions in future.

'To a medical Surgeon maybe Mistress.' His answer came in kindly understanding.

'What is the fate of those who survive Armand, do they know this location?'

'They go free Mistress. Your husband has insisted on the principle that those who win their lives keep them. It is the duty of our staff to make sure each one is transferred far away where they will not be found. And, no, they have been brought here in sealed carriages'

'This night we have six more pairs of men before the last; those are prisoners taken in war.' Armand informed. 'The duration must end before dawn. Every trace of the night's action has to be eradicated before it is light.'

The following bouts were between convicts, some masked as was their wish. Now the acts became more gross attaining total decapitation of the opponent or death by another method, but no weapons were allowed. The garrulous crowd called for disembowelling and 'take his head off.' It seemed anything should be permitted to get more aroused pleasure.

An interval was heralded by bright lights, causing a release of high pitched squeals anticipating other pleasures and indulgence to come. Not so amongst the low level onlookers. They moved away back into deeper shadowy groups.

'Will you walk amongst the spectators Mistress?'

'Oh no Armand, I don't know if I will ever avail myself of that honour.'

He smiled at my sarcasm.

I retired to an anteroom to be served with hot chocolat.

I felt exhausted as I sat listening to the people below. The voices made a medley of muffled sounds around the circular building.

Armand waited outside the door giving me time for private thought before I beckoned him in.

'Do we provide the refreshments in the salons Armand?' I asked.

'Yes Mistress. We never allow outsiders to have any method to infiltrate. 'We also sell items of high value jewellery and gems. I must tell you it was wise of you not to mingle with the audience, especially in the balcony. Between bouts some indulge in acts of gross indecency as the evening progresses.'

'But then surely that's what they pay for Armand, the ability to practice in public to a willing clientele. Am I not right?'

'You are Mistress.'

'You see I have witnessed a measure of humanity in freedom and at ease with their situations during my travels.' It was obvious Philippe had been discrete in not fully revealing my background. Armand would be surprised at what my fellow artists and I had seen from the high trapeze when we sat at rest above the high wire between our sessions.' I wasn't however prepared for this finale.

'There will be two last bouts tonight Mistress, each come with the Emperor's own specific commands.'

When the company had returned to their seats and the upper level had regained a modicum of composure, Armand pointed out that among the dark onlookers were six Marshalls. These men had brought the prisoners. 'These four men have been offered the chance to gain their freedom' he said.

'Prisoners?' I quizzed.

'From the Emporer's campaign spies – maybe double Agents, who knows?' He replied, 'Now you will see your husband's inherited duty.'

'My husband, but he is no longer.'

'No Mistress, not him. Not tonight, his second has taken that position this night.'

The lights found their pin point in the darkened arena picking out two men where they stood still; both quite naked except one wore a black head and eye mask. Quick intakes of breath came from all sides.

'That is from visitors,' Armand indicated, 'our members would know what to expect.' Now I noticed some figures stood up amongst the audience in the lower level. 'Those are Marshals who have brought the prisoners.' Armand explained.

The two men came forward and proceeded to wrestle with furious meaning.

'This can only be to the death of one at the Emperor's decree.'

'But he doesn't know that, from how you explained he has been given the opportunity to fight for his life.'

'Yes, that is so. For these it is different.'

Before the audience got more and more wild, erotically spurring on the prisoner's growing agony the man in the mask deftly broke his opponent's neck, saluted the corpse and walked away. A deep exhale of breath ensued.

'Armand, did I see what I thought I saw?'

'You did Mistress.'

I had to know it all, cruel and unjust as it was. I had noticed one of the Emperor's Marshalls raised his white gloved hand; was it a sign to take the life of the prisoner I wondered?

'The Master was a swift fighter and knew his timing exactly but this second was hesitating the Marshall saw it and signalled a swift finish.' Armand explained.

I found myself giving an involuntary shudder at the reason why my husband had kept his body so well tuned.

During our exchange figures in the crowd were vigorously rising, holding their white numbers up high, stretching to achieve better recognition.

This time the rowdy crowd had disappointment to shout about when a number on the lower level won the auction.

'That number goes to an experimental physician Mistress.' I was informed; immediately bringing to my memory that I had come across one of those before.

The next time my husband's second came out he performed his duty so swiftly the crowd in the gallery rasped their disapproval at the curtailed excitement.

'Now this is the last bout, they are two Russians who have won the right to fight for life against each other.'

Great anticipation rippled through the balcony. Those eager to see most in the audience surged forward to the front seats nobody able to hold them back.

A steward completely covered in black except for his mouth and chin came to the centre of the arena. All went quiet.

'Members and guests will please be seated' he ordered.

Reluctantly everybody returned to their seats. He was unmoving until everyone was re-seated.

'No person will leave their seat until this bout is over and the ring cleared.'

Armand whispered, 'We now have to avoid a rush to the exit and the holding area to allow the last winner is safely secreted away.'

Two unmasked men came through opposite gates. Both were naked. One had a fine tall muscular body the other was heavy yet not fat or flabby. I had the feeling this was going to be a gruelling spectacle and hoped it would not be too lengthy.

The steward called the men to the centre and spoke quietly to them both.

'He is telling them, in their own language, that when one sees his moment he must administer a swift death. Prolonged agony will not be tolerated or the killer will be cut down and the victim set free.'

At first the men stalked each other before the heavier man quite calmly turned his back on his opponent and walked away preening himself to the crowd sending them wild. The two Marshalls standing were joined by the other four, ready for action. The man laughed at them and moved on. The tall one was wary and wisely so for the heavy stalker suddenly swung his body around and with amazing agility flew at his opponent who for a bare second didn't move then deftly at the last moment side stepped leaving the fast moving body to go hurtling past – except that the body did not, for the tall man had flicked out his foot tripping the heavy body towards the floor. The upper man brought himself firmly down on to the prone man and with one hand dug his fingers deep into his adversary's neck muscles taking his life in an instant.

The winner stood tall, breathing heavily then went to move away and was at once impeded by two stewards and made to be still. They did not touch him. The referee bent on one knee and putting his hand to the neck of the horizontal figure pronounced him dead. Bedlam broke out but immediately silenced. The victor had disappeared from view amongst the flying black cloaks, escorted to safety, the loser remaining untouched. The referee scanned the crowd for those figures he'd been briefed were the owners of the dead man's body. They were I was told either his relatives or Russian agents. 'We did not enquire.' Armand said.

Their numbers were pointed out and three people descended, this time down into the arena and proceeded to wrap the body in a great cloak before leaving through the private entrance.

The crowd were allowed to relieve their stoked up tensions at full tilt. As long as all was cleared by the light of dawn nobody hindered their party spirits. It was better, Armand informed me for their safety they wind down before taking to the road and countryside.

The night was not over for me however. I was taken to meet the duty staff down in the area around the arena. This is where Philippe would have finished the evening's events. I thanked our staff and wished them all a good night until noonday when we had planned to gather all the staff together.

Armand took me through the exit passage into my private courtyard. As we walked across to the house Philippe's two Irish hounds fell in step either side of me. They instinctively seemed to know now that I had taken their Master's place.

As I entered my apartments the hounds laid down across the entrance.

Before Armand left me he handed me yet another envelope.

This time the letter had to wait.

* * * *

The door closed behind me. I could do nothing to control my heaving stomach. Vomit was the least of it. My body reacted violently to everything I had experienced.

Whatever those people had done the injustice of their endings especially the cold blooded murder angered me. Once I could have been in their position. No say in the matter of my fate.

It took hours before my body ceased its emotional upheaval. I couldn't give in to sleep. Before dawn I dressed in a pair of Philippe's riding breeches and a loose shirt. I didn't need anything on my feet. There was nobody awake in the stables when I walked Philippe's horse Blade into the yard. Nuzzling my loose flowing hair and clothes the animal was at first confused but comforted by the two hounds in close attendance. Gripping his mane I rode bareback across the park. The rhythmic thudding of the horse's hooves had such a soothing effect. Harder, harder, I needed to urge my steed up the escarpment onto the plateau where I had first viewed Philippe's chateau, now my home. Faster and faster across the fine turf kicking up great clods of earth. My hair whipping wildly across my face cut the skin but I didn't care, the more pain the better. I had the need to suffer.

The hounds had dropped back and lay in wait while Blade and I ran on. Looking back I could see how the hounds had edged forward to where I was always within the view of at least one of the loyal animals.

Both my mount and I revelled in the early morning gallop.

Whilst he enjoyed the freedom from saddle and bridle our physical connection enabled me to purge some of the human horror out of my body. Nevertheless I had to think and act sensibly. So I turned the brave animal. No good ruining his health thoughtlessly by my own selfish need. I hoped myself purged of all emotion, but no, anger still flowed through me.

Whatever Philippe's instructions he had noted the decision to participate was mine, and I had to make that decision soon, before the noonday meeting for all those it would affect.

Last night's action had not been a complete revelation but now I had the feeling I was falling into an abyss. I knew by all the secrecy there had to be much more. Philippe had already drawn the lines and was beginning to fill the colour of events but what colour? To my mind it was only black coldness. I could not administer this compassionless killing for a homicidal maniac coupled with the perverted gaiety from the Gross Theatre Macabre audience.

How did I want to lead my life? I saw my journey was at a fresh turning point. Maybe even into the fourth quarter of my time.

Dropping down from Blade's back I was met out in the stable yard by my tearful maid.

'Oh madam,' she wailed, 'Armand has near whipped me for not keeping track of you. Not looking after you. There's a messenger arrived and nothing can happen until you were found.'

Armand was horrified to see my garb and my body still running with sweat in Philippe's shirt and breeches clinging, drying against my skin. No shoes and hair flung wildly down my back. Lucy threw the robe she had been clutching around my shoulders and fought beneath its flowing length to cover my feet in a pair of elegant slippers. Armand supported the girl's efforts with,

'Madam, the Marshall would be scandalised to see you thus. Please.'

With Philippe's two hounds so close I could feel their rough coats feather against my legs, Bundzao, now the oldest keeping ground behind as I walked across the hall. Armand quietly calling the animals back.

'No, let them be. They know their duty Armand.' Staying close the hounds did not hesitate.

The Marshall, although looking askance at my dishabille, asked to speak to me alone. He spoke his message then rode away. What he told me made my resolve simple.

'Armand,' I ordered, 'gather all the servants together here at once, male and female if you please.'

It took a while to summon everybody from around the buildings and grounds but I was prepared, nay, thankful to wait, to think.

The message was pivot to lifting the weight from my shoulders.

Standing, my head and feet bare, I had kicked the silly shoes away. I was still drenched in half dry sweat from the vigorous ride. Now breathing deeply I felt my inside smiling.

'I am informed,' I told the company, 'the Emperor has been forced to abdicate and is now being taken into captivity. The events in the arena will cease from today.'

My words were met with stunned silence.

'Armand will be informing you how we will proceed. Meanwhile we will all put our minds on my husband's funeral.'

I knew that if the Emperor's changed circumstances had not come to my rescue I would have had a tremendous battle with Armand and the Establishment.

As Philippe warned me, establish firm control let nobody get the upper hand. I had decided on my returning ride that I did not want any involvement in cold blooded murder. Now the responsibility for the demise of such events had passed from my hands, I still needed to move fast to slip the bonds because political situations could change about just as swiftly. Many would not be suppressed by this setback.

Sky watching was another matter. The pursuit of scientific interests would go on. Their world could be dangerous but I hoped, not murderous.

I did read Philippe's last letter.

I had loved the man that was my husband but I could not love this man's persuasion.

* * * *

Although a huge burden had been removed from my shoulders I
still had, as Countess Carlotta d'Ville McGuire, the responsibility
of disposing of the services and the servers. I had a duty to preside
over the restructuring of the family business empire to maintain and
rebuild a valuable inheritance for Isabella and protect the authority
in the structure and lands inherited by Philippe's two sons.

Now it was my sad duty to write to Isabella and the boys. I
decided I would write to each, their own letter; after all they may at
the time my news arrives be in different parts of their islands, and
their father had a personal relationship with each one of his children.

* * * *

With the aid of Armand I had to emphasise a new focus to the
building. Re-group the staff and reallocate their time. I felt
responsible for their livelihood and families.

After Philippe's burial the candles burned long into the night as
I worked in my bedchamber. There were so many secrets remaining
in the strong boxes to be sifted through. I had my own personal
need to maintain my own privacy. Not even my maid had ever seen
what was hidden behind my eye patch. No gossip amongst the staff
ever came near the truth. Not being born in France knowledge of
my early years had not followed me.

Solitude was my protector. When Lucy had completed my
toilette and cleared away my clothing she would bring from the
kitchen fresh hot water to replenish my small samovar and a tray
containing chocolat and my Trembleur. This was our nightly
routine. She withdrew and I closed my door behind her.

Before starting my writing I made my first cup of chocolat, a
friend and comforter.

* * * *

Beside my dear Trembleur, a friend from my early days in France,
sat the small silver box Philippe gave me replenished regularly with

my one real indulgence, darkest powdered chocolat from South America. I used it now in these busy evenings, to give me strength while I read and translated documents long into the night.

This particular evening only one candle stood on the desk giving just enough light for writing, the shadows, in the far corners of the room were deep and dark.

I removed the cover from my eye allowing me a wider breadth of vision letting my pen speed across the paper with greater freedom, as time went by I felt composure flow back into my head and down through my body. For a while I sighed into the peaceful quiet of the night. Suddenly a movement from across the room caught my eyes as it reflected on the glass of Philippe's miniature portrait standing at the back of the desk, as ever my action to cover my eye was swift and without a pause I stood and turned facing the window to where a figure was just entering from the veranda. He stood motionless straight and tall between the heavy curtains both of us looking directly at one another through the softly lit space. I knew who it was immediately, he surveying me I waiting on his first move. A deep voice penetrated the air between us,

'Hallo Suzanne, I knew that must be you at the burial service, Oh, my apologies, Madam the Countess Carlotta.' He said making a low sweeping bow, 'It's been a long time.' He glanced around into the shadows. 'I thought you'd do well in your life, but this looks very well. And you,' I did not speak, the next second he was standing up close in front of me seeming to have moved in a blink of an eyelid but only as I would have expected, 'are now a beautiful widow no longer the child I knew.'

'You are no longer the boy I knew. Although still lithesome I see.' Tall, full of animal attraction, all of those, the image of his father Paul, but more, he had leaped across the room like a ballet dancer, and now we both stood hard straight, nearly touching. Slowly he raised his hands to my bare shoulders. Long smooth fingers lay on the edge of my dress. It was no good I felt an unexpected quiver go down my spine as he jerked me against the edge of the desk. But he hadn't pushed me. This man, calling me by another name, slowly, gently lowered his head to kiss my neck pushing my dress further down as he touched his lips across to my shoulder tip. I still said nothing, made no movement I knew him so well I let him kiss me intimately on the mouth. No man other than my husband had been in my bedroom before; no man other than Philippe had got further than the bottom stair. Now this man was pushing my dressing coat slowly off my shoulders slipping the white silk camisole down to my cleavage.

'Still the eye patch, but now oh so delicate and chic. In all those years I've never seen your eye.' his still low murmuring voice cajoled, 'Let me see your secret now my darling.' His fingers fluttered up across my shoulder, neck, cheek towards the black silk patch. Startled at the sight that met his eyes he pulled away better to see this revelation so close after so many years of wondering, a frown furrowed his brow.

'But I don't understand it's magnificent.' He paused, 'to have one beautiful dark golden eye is luck but to have a pair of blue irises like two lovebirds is a gift beyond the imagination.'

His attention changed in an instant aggressively pressing my body back kissing me hungrily handling me as if they belonged to him.

'I've longed for you all my life Suzanne and now you are free?' I had to be decisive, keep the upper hand.

'That's enough no further. I will choose who I take as a Lover.' I told him. As I turned away from my intruder a sly look came into his eyes. I was so angry with what he presumed were my grieving widow's needs I raised my voice, in answer, a low growl came from the other side of my door, 'You know well Suzanne has not existed since the first night I came to your parents van, we were only children then.' His fingernails dug into my shoulders and sly turned to a smirk. I stiffened under his grasp and put on a firmer tone, 'The brethren would not expect you to betray a sister. Now go Vincent, and please don't come again.' I did not want him hanging around. He bent to close in on me, when claws scrabbling to gain hold on the shiny floor, heralded Bunzoe's daughter Zowe as she came slowly through the curtains from the balcony snarling with low intent. Immediately my door handle cracked down and Bunzoe stood at her full height.

'As you wish,' he smiled, blew a kiss and went the way he had
come. Vincent was well aware of his beauteous body, it was his
living. I remember how he danced on the high wire and flirted with
the trapeze. The hounds could have ruined all that.

The next morning I ordered lockable fine mesh screen doors
made to fit all the doors and windows on the first floor.

If it wasn't him, of whom I knew of old, at least I had been
forewarned of the danger a widow could attract and besides, in
my bedroom I held all the damning documented evidence of the
'service', so called, that had been done in the name of the Emperor.
The chateau housed gold and more besides under the guise of a club
for wealthy men. After all, Vincent could have been another of those
double agents. How could I know? I had to keep the upper hand as
Philippe had warned. Much had to be disposed of in the following
days before I could turn my attention to the gentlemen's club when
that operation would shed all its secrets.

Now you know Carlotta's secret
please keep it to yourself
let new readers learn the
secret when they read this book!

* * * *

Blessed relief arrived in a carriage bringing Sally who, hardly taking
a breath, came in saying, as luck would have it my note telling her
of Philippe's demise reached Elsa's farmhouse the day before she
had planned to leave for England to visit Amy and the family. So
here she was, arms out stretched embracing me in a loving sister's
greeting. Oh, didn't we gossip and laugh. What a wonderful
distraction from all my cares and responsibilities, all washed away,
for a while.. In the midst of our conversation Sally said,

'Ah now I've just remembered something. We passed a rider
on the road this morning riding hard passed us in the opposite
direction and I felt sure it was Vincent.' For a moment I felt shocked
because it was three nights since I sent him away. Sally obviously
saw my surprise, remarking, 'He could not have recognised me,

I had my face covered away from all the dust coming into the carriage.'

I told her he had been here and everything that happened. Within the hour I heard from Armand that the problem with my intruder had in fact been dealt with by my watchful men servants.

'The gentleman will never return.' Armand reassured me in his usual positive tone. I did not ask for details.

Sally stayed for a month helping to lighten my load. While I met with a group who represented the club members and the male servants who in practice ran the operations, I was nevertheless the head of the family and had the final say. There would always be influential men of all persuasions who wanted a place in privacy to practice their mores. On our side it was a business that was my responsibility to keep earning wealth for our children. Dear Sally somehow her presence seemed to make life run smoothly again.

Although I was reluctant to see her leave Sally had been on her way to England to visit Amy and the family and so regretfully I had to let her go. I hadn't met with Amy for many years but I had always kept in touch. She was the closest to a Grandmother I never had.

Martha closed the little book saying that it was the last entry Carlotta left us in this diary. Now it's Sally's letters that tell us more about Amy's life. I'll read you some. Her hand writing is so beautiful and easy to read.

PREQUEL: 1765 – 1889

25

Sally recalls events in her letters to Elsa and Helene in France

'I was reluctant to leave Carlotta, she'd had such a huge responsibility thrust upon her; besides the obvious fact she would now be a target for any oversexed male looking to gain more than just a wealthy woman. However I knew she was a strong determined character and of course the way she had seen Vincent off proved she would always be her own woman. No, perhaps I should not worry. I had wanted to be in England in good time for my Mother's sixtieth birthday but after staying with Carlotta I only managed to get there with just a day to spare. Sixty years seemed a great age but Mum seemed as young and busy as ever. Tom hadn't worked full time in the carpenter's shop since a sharp splinter pierced his eye rendering him blind in that eye. On my arrival I found Tom had lost the sight in the other eye and was reduced to whittling toys from wood off cuts. My three step brothers, Joseph, Edwin and James, worked the family Carpenter's business making and repairing furniture; with James, the youngest, turning his skills more to finer smaller items; like tea boxes and ladies personal travelling caskets. George, Tom's son from his first wife, had taken over her father's Blacksmith's Forge some time back; he was a great bear of a man full of energy and strength. James was married to a lovely part Spanish girl. The other three boys hadn't married. Mother still collected herbs making salves and lotions, for there was always the need. She was known for miles around for her soothing liniments. There was something else she had become known for and that was her China collection. For some reason I had not told Carlotta about James' great find back in 1802. I think I must have been away travelling and when we met again in '07 for that first night at the Regent's Theatre Royal in Brighton, my mind was much more involved in introducing Carlotta and Philippe to my friend Maria Fitzherbert, that afterward we had so much other gossip to fill our short visit that personal family news never entered the conversation.

In her next letter Sally says, Now that I have time, I'll tell you how Mother's china collection came about.

As I mentioned, it was in 1802. That winter there were so many great raging storms along the low Sussex coast, the Shore men were constantly out watching every night for signs of rough high water running up Channel, so they soon knew when there was likely to be wrecks in the bay. My brother James was only sixteen at the time and like all young men he looked out for excitement, leave alone the chance he might spot Boney's men trying their luck at our shores. Well it was second nature for people along the shore to keep watch, when vessels past the high chalk cliff at Beachy Head. The waves swept boats across Anderida bay where the sea bed looks smooth, but stumps of an ancient forest; some say five thousand years old, showed like treacherous grinning teeth at low tide. It was well known locally that many more patches of old tree stumps spread far out into the Channel.

A floundering ship is often first located by sound. It's the high pitched siren of dogs barking their warnings as an oncoming vessel, pushed by the wind up Channel, nears their own shore. By the early hours of the night I'm telling about, groups of men and women had gathered in readiness alongside their many carts in silent anticipation. Sheltering behind the dunes from the blasting gale, James called it a long black furious night before he was the first to pick out the white water rip round a ship's bow near to their shore. That's when they knew there would not be much longer to wait. Rich rewards come from patient waiting. What is a catastrophe to some is the living for others. It's all part of the Marsh and farmland life where the low foreshores boarder the land. Wrecks to landsmen are the harvest of the sea. When the time arrives all is gathered in. Nothing wasted. The waters along the far eastern coast of Sussex are shallow. Wide expanses of deep soft sandy mud lures and sucks ships into its depth.

There are always a few locals who, down the generations, keep the knowledge of the pathways below the waterline, to venture out some distance, to render help to stranded sailors. Known as Life

Shoremen they are the only ones who enter the wrecks to save lives whilst in great danger of losing their own. Otherwise people wait for goods to be flung up by the fury of the waves or float ashore on the incoming tide. Ships timbers have always been much prized by our family. Anything that drifts in on the tide is flotsam, whilst the items jettisoned to lighten a ship that finally fetches up and stops on shore is jetsam. Both legal finds. Those locals quick off the mark make early gains and they get back away home fast.

That night James made many good finds and was about to set off back to father's workshop, when he noticed a substantial slatted wooden box well up into the long sea grass. He could see it had been hurled in at great force, by the damage it had suffered; windings of plaited straw poked out from the split slats. James has an eye for good pieces of timber so he decided to investigate and found the main struts were worth having but when he tried to move the crate it was unusually heavy. Pulling aside the swags of plaited straw he could see shining blue and white porcelain china. Very saleable, he thought, and worth making the extra effort to bring his horse and cart around as far as he dared for he was already full laden. It took some time to finally get his load home but when he wrenched the crate timbers apart he found quantities of tightly packed tea-ware, meat chargers, flat dinner plates and more. Deep inside finely pierced edge compote tureens and serving dishes snuggled unblemished. Coming out from the dark depth of the forge to see what was glittering in the sunshine, George immediately recognised the pattern, he having seen the very same blue and white pattern china, when he had been over to Brighthelmstone some months before, delivering his pair of wrought iron gates. He told the family the blue and white was called Willow pattern.

James thought it would be wonderful for mother to choose first and of course Ma was unable to part with such a beautiful collection. She ended up keeping a great many pieces, "To pass on to the family." She said meaning, "You will all need dishes when you marry." Anyway that was her excuse. The few pieces Ma rejected James took to market. He had hoped to take more than just a small amount of china to sell, but Tom had a quiet word, telling James, 'What you are taking is enough, as it was best not to draw attention, for it could be thought the family should be paying an extra tithe.'

Mother told me it wasn't until she was putting one or two of the most delicate pieces away, for gifts she hoped to give to the boys' future brides, when she came across your parcel Elsa, the one you pushed into Ma's horse's pannier bags when we fled from Cakebread.

'You know, I couldn't believe my eyes,' Ma said, 'with all the turmoil at the time and then leaving you at Moat Mount with Suzannah, that little parcel went straight out of my mind. When I opened it what do you think I found?' She pointed to the shelves on the wall Tom had made for the Willow pattern plates. Among them were the two leaf shaped dishes you two had used on your meal table. Mother laughed saying, 'Well Sally my love, do you remember what you used to call those two dishes?'

'Of course,' I remembered them immediately, 'Ginger and Pickles.' I cried.

'Yes and look they're the same Willow pattern, a reminder of my two lovely sisters. How are those dear girls?' Mum asked, because she hadn't seen you since you left England. I had to tell her that you, Helen, are in great good health, still working on the family farm, but that you, Elsa, you are not so robust although refusing to be a burden, you fill your days by knitting for Helen and Paul's Grandchildren.'

'This is the last of Sally's letters.' Martha said, as she folded the pages and slipped them back into the Bowler Hat box. 'You know we had some lovely long conversations, Amy, Sally an me. Sally found the greatest enjoyment on her travels, was to be allowed into the workshops and homes of craftsmen making things. On one of the earliest visits back to Sussex she brought a gloriously bright shawl from Spain for my Rosanna. It set her shining black hair off so well. She knew James was keen on Rosanne but was too shy in those days to ask for her. Oh yes, Sally was ever thoughtful of the family, this time she had brought me a cuckoo clock from a village in the Alps and a parcel of small wood off cuts from a workshop of makers of stringed instruments. Edwin, Amy's second son, was never very strong; but he was nevertheless a skilful craftsman. He made beautiful inlaid boxes working up in the sunny space above the carpentry where her mother and sisters first had their weaving looms when hiding away from Cakebread..

Martha then told us that Sally had only been home for a month with Amy and the family, when a letter arrived from Carlotta to say her daughter Isabella, had come home from her travels saying she intended to marry an Englishman, a Lawyer named Mr William Winterton. So Carlotta was planning to host a wedding in the not too distant future. Martha chuckled knowingly,

'Typical Sally,' she said, 'there she was again; full of excitement to be off on another adventure. 'I'll go over to Brighhelmst'n. Last time I was there I saw a young Silversmith. He was making fine tableware, just right for a wedding gift. Ah, and it will give me the opportunity to meet some old friends.' Yes typical Sally.' Martha sighed, and just, fell asleep.

'Well after all she was 105.' My mother said."

When Clara paused, Artie commented that Sally and her friends certainly travelled about a lot even though, in those days, the roads must have been pretty rough? Clara agreed, but she had learned there was a very good stage coach service that kept to the edge of the chalk Downs, just up off the marsh lands.

"Now, my story doesn't finish there. The most important part is still to come. But I do need a breather." While Clara had a short rest, Artie shovelled a second bucket of coal on the fire before the company settled back for next part of the story.

PREQUEL: 1765 – 1889

26

James takes over the story

When Clara started again she said, "Mum told me Martha had fallen into a deep slumber so Amy's eldest son James, who then must have been in his seventies, told us the final story. As he said, he had witnessed what happened.

'This was not long after Sally had left to go over to Brighthelmstone. Amy, as was her usual way, had gone out in the early sunny summer morning, collecting herbs for the family pot. There was a place she knew up on the hill where Good King Henry and Sorrel grew. As her story goes, she had picked two lovely bunches and was just shaking off the last sparkling drops of dew, thinking to herself how the years were making her movements stiff; she was reminded of Tom saying she should straighten her back slowly, when suddenly her thoughts were cut short. Across the field below where she stood, the pathway curved back on itself. She told how she saw a figure hunched up against the hedge over which he was leaning with what looked like a spy glass to his eye. Amy first thought it was that chap Will Turner the Artist, back again with his drawing book; but when she drew herself up to her full height she could see the figure was bigger and heavier than Will. Nobody frequented the pathways around the village that she didn't know by sight; she would recognise at a glance any one of the villagers working away in the fields. She didn't know this man. He appeared quite old, and why, she thought, was he looking so intently through a glass? Following the angle of his spy glass pointing towards the village, she could see only but a few figures moving at this early hour. Four men were out in the surrounding fields but he wasn't looking that far. Turning back to him she followed his line of sight again and noticed Martha was throwing her bedding out over the bedroom windowsill to air, then young Rosanna, came into view returning from the midden with the night bucket, but the telescope wasn't aimed their way. When she turned again to look at the stranger the figure had disappeared. Instead of carrying on her usual route she turned and retraced her steps unable to quell the niggling feeling that seemed to be rising deep in her chest. Looking down over a lower hedge she saw Tom was now on his stool out in the yard working at the knob to decorate a Bannister for the Charlton's new Manor House. Ah, dear Tom sitting there so calm in the morning sunshine. She almost tripped and saved herself in time. Her foot was caught in the fold of an oiled cloth poking out from beneath the hedge. It was something like a seaman would have. Momentarily her heart came up into her mouth she hadn't noticed it on her way passed. Suspicion made the hair on the back of her neck stand up. Was it a ground sheet for sleeping? Her feet could hardly keep up with her need to move on faster downward. As she entered the house I had just come in from my early morning jobs and had the old iron pan over a bright red fire and was dropping my first egg into hot bacon fat. Through the kitchen window Amy caught sight of the figure sideways on to her and hunkered down beside Tom; both men seemed to be deep in conversation. As she watched the stranger's right hand came up onto Tom's shoulder, it had no thumb, an instant later she saw his left hand flip his coat tail as if to reach into his waistband for a knife. In a flash she knew who it was, without looking she grabbed hold the handle of the frying pan and was out of the back door leaving me holding two halves of an egg shell its contents splattering amongst the coals. I had to duck a shade to look through the window; watching, I was astounded to see how fast my usually calm gentle mother of over sixty years, was sprinting as swiftly as any eighteen year old across the yard, and to my horror I saw her swing the heavy pan high above her head and bring it down in both hands with a thrashing crash. The stranger's head split. The body slumped, an egg slithering down its back. Tom jumped up off his stool away from the noise making no sound of his own. The pan clattered heavily onto the cobblestones. No more thoughts as to why and how; I leaped out through the back door snatching up my cloak intending to throw it round Ma's shoulders but she was already enclosed in father's arms. Looking down at the body I saw a head almost cloven free from a body and twisted half round where a sharp sheath knife lay shining rudely in the sunlight on the palm of the left hand. All doubt of the living man's intention gone. Then, oh god, heavy footfalls came rounding the end of the house. Thank goodness it was George. He stopped in his tracks and did I let out a sigh of relief. I threw my cloak over the body but not before George's gasp of recognition almost said its name.

'That's not? It can't be.' Ma nodded. All eyes rested on the cloak shrouded heap except Tom's of course, who broke the pause,

'I had just caught the smell of him. I knew I was right when I heard the thwack.' I had heard Joseph come into the kitchen behind me as I ran to help Mother, and he came across the yard saying,

'It's the Lime pit for him.' Nobody stopped to question our mother there was no need. We heaved the bundle on board Joe's wagon and he drove away to work as he normally did saying he was early, there wouldn't be anybody about yet and not to come with him, that would look unusual. I took the knife away but not before Amy gently touched my arm and told me about the cloth she had seen in the hedge, I said he would take care of it. When we all came in round the supper table that evening Joseph reported the man had one empty eye socket and his right hand was without a thumb. Amy's only comment was,

'If I had given it a moment's thought Tom would be dead.'

She knew more than anyone else how ruthless that man could be, he had no conscience. Tom said, 'If he had carried his hate all these years he would never have stopped now.' James took a long pause, "My goodness that was another whole life time away.' "

Clara closed her eyes and folded her hands together, quite spent. A huge sigh of relief and shock exploded from her listeners defused by Artie, saying,

"Well, that's what I call a crackin' good yarn."

Clara gave him a wry smile.

PREQUEL: 1765 – 1889

Postscript

"Late as it is," Dolly announced, "we need a reviver before home. I'm going to make us a pot of tea. "

"Woo lovely." Clara sighed.

Out in the kitchen putting the kettle on and setting out a plate of biscuits Dolly could hear the murmur of voices coming from the front room. Yes, she knew their curiosity was getting the better of them there were too many unanswered questions. Although Dolly knew her mother was tired, Clara was enjoying every moment of her story telling, and always had so much to tell. It could well be the last time the family would get together for a while.

As Jimmie came through the kitchen door to lift the tea tray up the stairs for Dolly he said, "That's not an old bowler hat box; they didn't wear bowler hats in Amy's days?" "No your right Jim," Dolly answered, "mum just liked to call it a bowler hat box. I expect it was more likely used for wigs in the seventeen hundreds."

Revived as she sipped her tea from her beloved old tea dish more details came back into her mind once again.

"You know Amy never did tell Sally how she came to be married to Abel Cakebread. Even when her daughter asked how she got the nasty scar on her ankle. None of it was Sally's fault and she had as a very little child loved her father. No, Amy did not want Sally to feel guilty."

"Didn't she know about Cakebread's reappearance?"Artie asked.

"If you remember, Sally had gone over to Brighton. The family were relieved she wasn't there; and they decided it best she was never informed."

"This lady Carlotta made quite an impression on you didn't she Ma?' Jimmie commented.

"I know I was only four years old but I do remember seeing her at Amy's funeral. She wasn't dressed in black like everybody else?" I had to ask my mother about Carlotta because she looked so unusual."

'What a memory you have.' Mother said, 'Yes she was not like anybody at the funeral at all. It was the first time that any of us had met Carlotta she must have been over eighty years old at the time. And it was the only time she came to the Lamb Inn. She sat talking with John and Annie for a long time.'

"So then did Carlotta hear about Amy's story too?" Hilda asked.

"No, James waited 'til everybody had left, he wanted only us to know because it was an important event in our family's life and should be handed down privately in the family." Then Jim asked,

"Didn't Martha know then, after all she was Amy's oldest friend?"

"Oh yes, she knew." Clara said, "She and her daughter Rosanne were there in the village but my goodness, they were sworn to secrecy. It would never have done to let even a whiff of what happened at the time; you know how Martha loved to talk. This was the one thing she did keep to herself. Well of course until after Amy's funeral when she was finally annoyed into telling the truth."

'And what about Sally, wasn't she at her mother's funeral?' Hilda asked.

"No she died in about 1835. I say died but nobody in the family ever really found out exactly what happened. The last letter Amy received, James said, was when Sally was travelling with friends in Italy. It was Helen who wrote from France to tell Amy they hadn't received a letter from her for some while and asked if Amy had any news.

Sometime later Helen sent Amy the collection of letters Sally had written over the years to the family in France, for what she called Amy's memory box.

James said Sally was an unusually self possessed lady. She and her friend Carlotta seemed determined to run their own lives. Sally of course was a wealthy woman. She put some of her money into the farm Paul purchased so that they all had a permanent family home when they left the Circus. Elsa was already a widow so she and Sally moved in together. Then once Elsa was settled Sally went off on her travels again. When Elsa's health began to fail, Helen and Paul gave up the Circus life and joined Elsa. The farm was Sally's home base so she returned there whenever she felt like a rest. That's the way

Helen described her niece's wanderings, and wander she did. She had friends in Vienna and travelled with them through Bohemia even to Constantinople. One time when she came back to England she'd been in the Alps and down into what she called the Peninsula. Helen received letters from Sally telling of the tours she and her friends made with local guides, sometimes visiting monasteries; many had guest houses. Her party never seemed to be in one place for very long, she certainly got about in her fifty years.

There was a last contact and that was a parcel. It arrived about a year after they had given up on hearing from her again. James couldn't remember the name of the place he said it came from, but it was addressed in an unknown hand to the, 'Hartshorn Carpenter Family,' and contained a lovely collection of pieces of unusual types of wood. Sally was always very thoughtful in the choice of gifts she brought home for each individual. It was like the similar package of wood she brought with her to England when she visited that time in 1808. James' brother Edwin was never so robust as the other boys so while they worked on house building and furniture making he turned his talents to producing fine inlaid boxes. Those first pieces of wood were acquired, Sally told Edwin, when she visited the workshop of a maker of stringed instruments in Switzerland. They were mostly quite small some only chips of wood but Edwin, he was really pleased with what she brought him. We supposed the parcel of wood that came was a collection she had been keeping for when she returned home on her next visit.'

'Sally gave Rosanne that beautiful rich swinging Shawl. Of course that was before she was James' wife. Sally said the bright colours made Rosanne's raven black hair look eve more glorious. She knew James was sweet on Rosanne and she must have decided it would be just the gift for a bride but took a lot longer to pluck up courage to ask for Rosanne.'

"When James was asked where Rosanne got her glossy black hair, commenting that everybody else in our family had gold coloured hair. Mum said James gave a chuckle, saying how Amy had told him Martha fell for a young man who travelled selling clocks. Apparently he swept her off her feet, but her old Dad, Bernie the village butcher, wouldn't let her go with him, Oh no, he told the chap if he was that keen he'd to come back for her when he came their way again, and he'd have to marry his daughter. The traveller did just that. Martha was a tall shapely golden haired gal and he was small and Latin with long black shining locks. The family thought he was a Spaniard but he and Martha didn't stay in the village long enough for anybody to find out before the couple ran away together. The next time the pair returned back home, Martha stayed with her parents to give birth to Rosanne while her husband went off on his travels around England delivering the clocks they had been across to Holland to buy. That was the last Martha saw of her husband. Whether he had an accident or was murdered nobody ever heard. Rosanne never knew her father. She grew up in the same village where Martha was born.

It was James who finally won her heart.'

'Rosanne was an unusual beauty she was dainty, like a high stepping pony with a flowing black mane olive skin and wearing that lovely shawl she made the men give more than a second look even when she was quite an old lady.'

"Well now you telling us about Rosanne most probably answers' the question I asked Dolly years ago." Artie said. Everybody looked across at Artie for his answer.

"Where did you and Jimmie get your jet black hair? You never had black hair did you Clara and Lily she's a blondie. But Hilda and Jim, their two, Don and Kathy they have black hair. Maybe it's been handed down from Rosanne?"

"You could be right there." Jimmie said, "I never thought of that, but this is the first we've heard of Rosanne and her father. Dolly and I always thought someone amongst our ancestors got involved with the ship wrecked sailors; those from the Spanish Armada queen Bess allowed to settle between the tide line and cliffs." Before that subject had time to expand Clara's mind had moved on.

"Oh and there's another little tid-bit my mother heard Martha mention at Amy's funeral. It was about her brother Jeb."

"'You mean the lad with the catapult whose aim never missed?" Dolly asked.

"That's right. Martha said Jeb went for a soldier after Amy got taken. He'd had his eye on her and he couldn't get over losing her. The family only saw him once when he came home for a visit before going with the Marines. The Admiralty got him aboard ship as a sharp shooter, so they said. Poor chap died at Trafalgar.'

'Yes Martha was Martha Watt before she got mixed up with that Victor Sebastiani. Amy and Martha were friends all their lives especially in their older years when Amy was a widow the two women were both too arthritic to sew and would sit talking, telling each other about the very private parts of their lives.

"The keepsakes in the old bowler hat box and Carlotta's diary together with Martha's memory gave us the sometimes harrowing yet remarkable story of Amy Hartshorn's life." It was Clara's last story, told at Christmas 1951.

I was there on that Christmas day evening. Being barely ten years old I recall just a few snippets of Granma's own words. But I do remember seeing the rolls of old letters and the diary; including a beautiful miniature portrait of Carlotta. That is how I knew exactly how to describe the unusual eye. Nobody had to tell me that, I saw it for myself. It was something one could not forget.

Then of course, with our family members being the way they are with their reminiscing and passing on family folk-lore, over the years I have gathered this tale into my memory store.

I do still have the box, although it is now in quite a sorry state having been up on the beams in our barn for many years. However, inside it retains its original bright blue painted surface. Sadly the letters, diary and miniature have disappeared.

Somebody else in the family probably have them somewhere?

Here is a taste of my next book

That's Not Funny!

Lilian Forshaw
An Autobiographical Memoir

Chapter One

August Bank Holiday 1951 our first family holiday and we were going abroad!

"We'd better see how much money I've saved." Mum brought out the old salt tin Dad had soldered shut in 1946, after Mum had been smooth talked by a distant relative who, my father said had, 'lost his shirt' on the horses, into 'lending' him all her savings, because the bookies were after him. Poor Mum, she had believed him and felt such a chump. "Never mind that's all in the past now Dolly." Dad put his soldering iron on the gas stove, to heat it up; 'til the tip sizzled sharply when you spat on it. When he ran the iron round the edge of the lid the solder slid off in a dribble of molten silver. Excitedly pulling the lid off Mum found she had saved twenty pounds, enough to pay the six pounds to rent the caravan for a week and pay for the train fares.

With the knowledge that Grandma was now happily in safe caring hands, Mum felt she was finally able to take a break.

I could hardly contain my excitement because we wouldn't have to wait until Saturday afternoon to start our holiday. The building firm my father worked for was closing down for the whole bank holiday week. It would be the first time Dad had finished work on Friday evening and had a two day weekend break.

By Friday afternoon Mum's big brown case, the one she said, *'used to carry everything I owned in that case;'* was packed, locked and standing in the hall. I'd overheard her count as she folded bed sheets, pillowcases, hand towels, night clothes and two sets of underwear for each of us; one on one off and one in the wash. Yet more excitement when Dad arrived home at six o'clock, carrying a big white china kitchen sink, hitched across his shoulder by a rope through its drain hole. It wasn't unusual to see him with such large and heavy items; what was unusual was that it was for us. And that wasn't all, perched on top of his tool bag, on his other shoulder was a mysterious looking lump inside a pillow case.

"Here's a nice new sink," he announced swinging it down onto the kitchen floor, "customer didn't want it sitting on the builder's rubbish out in the street for the neighbours to ogle. She asked me to take it away, said I could have it. I'll plumb it in when we get back from holiday." He added.

"You say she didn't want it?" Mum was incredulous, how could anybody throw away such a lovely deep sink.

"Ah well I've just put her in one of those new sink units, won't last as long as this would though."

While he was eating his evening meal it had always been father's way to tell us what he had been doing that day; where he had been working, who he'd met and what they'd said. This evening, when he finished eating he put his knife and fork together, pushed his plate away, said his usual, 'Thank you that was lovely Doll.' short for Dolly my Mum's family nick name. It had not past my notice that Dad had made no reference to the other parcel he had brought home that evening. Slowly he reached down beside his chair then, acting like he was a magician pulling a rabbit out of a hat, he lifted the old pillowcase high, pulled it open and revealed a small bright scarlet patent leather case.

"There now what do you think of that?" *Think*. All I could think was that I had never seen anything so gloriously glossy before in my life. When he snapped open the three stud fasteners that held the soft lid in place, we could see it had a pretty floral lining.

"Where ever did you get it from?" Mum asked.

"Remember that photo in the newspaper last week, the one of the little girl winning the silver cup for ice skating?" Mum shook her head, "You know," Dad insisted, "Publican's daughter at the Lathe Cleavers Arms, along Regent Row behind the Weston Road." he turned to me saying, "Her new skating boots won't fit in this case so she's sent it to you as a holiday gift." It didn't take me long to decide what I was going to use it for. My dolly Belinda would come on holiday too, she could look after my hair ribbons and bring all the new clothes our next door neighbour, Aunty Peerless, had made for her.

Before six o clock on Saturday morning the sun was flooding the kitchen with light. When Dad opened the back door the air slipped in around him soft and hot as if the gas oven had been turned on full blast,

"It's going to be a corker today." He remarked sitting down on the doorstep, beside his boot box, to polish his shoes.

"Right then," Mum said as she fidgeted tins of spam, corned beef and peas around a fruit cake, down into one of her shopping bags, lastly gently resting a brown paper bag with six new layed eggs on the top; a present from our neighbour. "Now we had better get a move on. I want your shaving kit and both of you go and get yu'r teeth cleaned, then I'll have your face flannels for the sponge bag, they're going in this small case with slippers and cardigans, it's likely to be chilly in the evenings by the sea shore."

Climbing back up the cellar steps she was saying, "That old meat safe down there's been a Godsend in this hot weather." Mum had cooked a shoulder of lamb when the oven was on last night for Dad's evening meal. Wrapping the meat with a thick layer of greaseproof and sheets of newspaper, she wedged the bundle between two screw top bottles, filled with cooled scalded milk, into the biggest of our weekend shopping bags, followed by a packet of Bisto and a cabbage. Laying newspaper in the bag on top of the tins, she piled in a heap of tiny new potatoes; two jars, one of pickles and one of jam, a packet of tea a bag of sugar and a loaf of bread. All this had to last us until the shops opened on Tuesday morning. She intended us to live in style. "Whoops better not forget, never know there might not be one there." she said to herself, slipping the tin opener into her hand bag. "Mm, that feels equal." Mum declared hefting the bags one each hand.

As Dad was carrying the cases out onto the front door step voices flowed on the warm air across the street,

161

"Have a good holiday." And "Bring us back a bucket of sand."
Neighbours passing by with their weekend shopping sounded Bank
holiday bright.

"Mines an ice cream cone," weezed Mr Lewis, walking by on
his way home from his night shift at the power station, "an' don't
let it dribble before I get it." he laughed.

"Fine chance" Dad quipped with his usual good humour.

"Best put your money on the bucket of sand for the kiddies."
Joked Uncle Bert, out on his doorstep giving his brass door-
knocker its daily polish.

"You ready Daw?" Dad called. Mum was sitting at the bottom of
the stairs easing on her new sandals. Wriggling her toes around she
stood up pulling her skirt this way and that making sure her seams
were straight. Dad had given her some nylons on Friday evening, he
said they were something special for the weekend that he got after
he'd had his hair cut at the Barber's in Cranbourne Street.

After pushing the big old iron key in the door lock Dad, went
back into the kitchen to make sure the gas was turned off and the
back door was locked. A ritual he did every time we all left the
house. Mum stood out on the pavement with a knowing smile on
her face while I, raring to go, hopped about between the cases
and the tall golden yellow daisies that overflowed the small front
garden. It seemed like an age before Father finally came walking
briskly out shutting the door behind him, the key turned in the lock
with the easy clunk of its years in use.

"Well, come on then." He said as if we had been keeping him
waiting. Short solid and strong my Dad threw his folded gabardine
rain mac over one shoulder, lifted the cases as if they were feather
pillows and strode off along the street towards the railway station.
Mum gave our neighbour a, 'would you believe it, 'eyes in the sky'
look, he replied with a knowing wink. They had all so recently come
through a war together and knew when to make allowances for
each other's little foibles, just like they knew everybody else's in the
street.

"Toodloo, have a good journey." Uncle Bert called.

"Bye Squire." Dad called back over his shoulder.

With her loaded shopping bags Mum had to give a little trot to catch up with Dad who had already started off at his regular easy pace. I, proudly carrying my beautiful red case skipped along by his side. No taxi riding for us, my parents didn't have that kind of money. More neighbours waved us on our way as we went down Stamford Road and along the Prestonville Road, Mum remarking to Dad,

"That's the first time I've got this young lady past the stained glass shop without her pleading to see inside."

"They're not there," I said, "there's no milk outside." It was the glint of light on all the colours through the windows at 'Barton Kinder and Alderson's,' that made me long to go inside to see their glass pictures; the fact I saw the empty milk crates outside told me there was nobody at work today. A few yards further along, high up on the corner of the garden wall behind the 'Good Companions' public house, a little wooden shed perched with a tree growing through its middle. Here was another place for my lingering, keen to see if any faces were peeping out of the tiny window. As we turned down to Howerd Terrace somebody called out,

"Lost yer way Artie boy?" before Dad could reply another voice answered,

"Nar, come on Bert get yer specs on, can't yer see 'is got 'is weasel* on 'is shoulder? He's off on 'is holidees."

Mum and Dad laughed Mum giving the joker a double shopping bag wave. I knew what Bert meant because my Father's usual route to work was across the Seven Dials and up over Dyke Road and down to the Clock Tower.

*Weasel – this was a joke referring to my father carrying his best rain coat – as if he had got it out of the pawn shop at the weekend to take it on his holiday. As in, 'Pop goes the weasel.'

Outside the Shakespear's Head in Chatham Place the Publican's wife was sweeping the steps, she called out, "Have a good time kids…," whispering something about not coming back with any buns in the oven. I didn't know why she said that because I knew Dad had made sure the gas oven was turned off before we left home, anyway I was too busy thinking of how I was going to show my shiny red case to my friend Julia; she lived in one of the funny pop bellied houses in Terminus Road, I knew if I ran my toe along the gratings in the pavement above her kitchen window she might look up and see me, then I could wave my case to her.

Smoke and coal smuts filled the air from the steam engines idling down below the cliff on the railway line. With only a few more steps to go down to the station, Dad was now exchanging cheery banter with the drivers waiting in their Taxis lined up beside the wall along the opposite side of the road, when two more heavily laden neighbours trudging by spoke to Dad, "'av a good holiday," they said in unison. Well! I thought everybody in the world must know my Father.

Inside the station we could hardly move between stacked cases and people gaggled in family groups. Older children were fielding squealing mobs of little kiddies skittering in all directions, round their parents dithering feet.

Dad knew we had to head for the platform on the far left for the Portsmouth train, so while Mum went to the ticket office, Dad found us a place in the queue.

"Train's in, we won't have to wait long." he told Mum when she caught up with us, her hands full of tickets and change. We didn't know anybody and nobody here knew us but everybody was talking to everybody else.

"This train right for Pompey mate?" a harassed looking man asked Dad,

"That's right." my Father replied. Immediately the man and his family became our chatty chums with a feeling of, we are all in it together.

When a Ticket collector opened the gates the crowd jerked heads up and forward as one. Cases and beach balls, parcels and cricket bats tripped shifting bodies causing sudden pushes and shoves spreading laughter that greased agitated nerves. The ticket collector shouted, "Order." Sharply slowing the easing bodies forward now in orderly file through the narrow gate.

Cutting his way through the melee on the platform, Dad found a corridor carriage, swung the large case up inside, before turning to help Mum into a corner seat, then hoisted the small case onto the rack above her head followed by the two shopping bags, but she refused to be parted from the bag containing the precious eggs. She held that safely on her lap.

My Father was always very caring and solicitous to Mum. Although I was only ten I knew Mum was feeling fragile and sometimes tearful; her hair was falling out leaving bald patches that she felt were so unsightly, and on top of all that she was worrying about Granma's failing sight. I heard our neighbour say it was all part of the stress left over from the war years and a good holiday would be, 'just the ticket.' However she didn't need a ticket to see the funny side of things. Thank goodness she still had her sense of humour because she needed it for what happened next.

"Phew, I didn't expect these new sandals would give me such gyp." Mum said. She was just slipping one sandal off when a rather stout lady, dressed in layers of bright yellow and orange summer frills; topped by a big floppy flowered sun hat, pushed her way into the compartment stepping on both Mum's feet. Amidst the, "Oh, sorry," flutters, giggles 'n' tutts, raising the temperature, Mum had no breath left to complain. It was Bank holiday after all and accidents will happen.

The train was filling fast so Dad and I retreated into the corridor where he made a space for me against the window beside our big case where I stood pinned, for the rest of the journey, while he stood behind me as a buffer against the bodies trying to squeeze along the narrow space that was left.

As the train moved off people got themselves comfortable where they stood; movement was limited but it wasn't all that bad because the holiday atmosphere was light hearted and jovial; elbows stuck in ribs followed by polite apologies; knees knocked knees provoking, by the sound of voices, naughty remarks, hushed away from children's ears. The air grew stifling, even though the corridor was on the shady side of the train. Soon there were pockets of jostling bodies, trying to remove layers of clothing. Most of our fellow passengers were wearing their Sunday best; women in summer dresses pulled off cardigans and waved their sun hats in their faces; men wearing sports jackets and flannels pushed their trilby hats to the backs of their heads to wipe their sweating foreheads; children sitting on piles of luggage were lifted even higher on top of their Father's rolled up macs. An anxious screeching voice called,

"Where's Jimmie?" Followed by a sad wailing child's,

"Hold my coat Mum. I'm tired."

Cheeky remarks gradually calmed and laughter rolled through the long tight space with good humour.

The railway line left Brighton station curving west along behind factories and people's back gardens. I enjoyed looking into back gardens, because it was like peeping into secret places you wouldn't normally see. Drawing in to Hove station more people ran along the platform searching for a space to squeeze in, meeting with shouts of,

"No room in 'ere mate." when,

"Just room for a small one." a man directed, opening the train door near us, drawing comments like,

"Oo-ER!" and

"What hoe?" from the occupants of our corridor, as all eyes followed a beautiful young blond tippy toeing along the platform on her high-heels,

"Here yew'ar love, up yer come." he called, holding his hand out to the girl. A woman behind him surrounded by small children said, "'e's a married man love." While another voice cut in, "Hands 'orf." causing a roar of good humoured laughter.

After this flurry of events the crowd settled down, it being cooler to keep quiet and watch the world go by. Their noses pressed against the windows, children's voices murmured, 'Tractor' and 'Sheep in that field,' one small voice piped up asking,

"Daddy, how can you tell a Bull from a Cow

An expectant silence hovered for a second then a great wave of hilarity burst out with adult jocularity, "Kiddies do say funny things." Somebody squawked, "Open that vent - pleeze - oh dear oh dear I can't breathe for laughing." Dad bent down and whispered in my ear,

"See all those big animals in that field they've got udders under their bellies. That's where the milk comes from - they're cows and look over there, that heavy ol' feller on his own. No udders, see? Well he's a Bull." I could always rely upon my Dad to tell the truth.

"But why are all those small cows running about?" I could have answered my own question before he said,

"Ar' they're little boys." I always saw boys as a big noise. The train was slowing down a porter's voice calling,

"Emsworth, Emsworth," that put a stop to the growing ribaldry only for our attention to be diverted by an awful shriek coming from the compartment behind us, where Mum was sitting. Before Father was able to turn to make sure Mum was alright we were pressed back by the turmoil of bodies rushing to fill vacated seats. Dad held on to me saying,

"We'll stay put, the next stop's ours. Not long now."

"Havant, Havaant." A slightly singsong voice called.

At last, our Station. It would be good to get out of the train, we were so hot. But first Dad had to negotiate our cases through the compartment between all the knees to reach the platform. Mum waited till we were on the platform before she stood up and carefully joined us still clutching the paper bag of precious eggs to her chest.

Having spent the journey on the north facing shady side of the train, the shock to our eyes was all the more dramatic; let alone the blazing heat reflecting back off the white sandy earth in the Station yard.

There was no shade at the place where we had to queue for the bus to take us on the last part of our journey; only another tangle of fishing nets buckets spades, folding and unfolding push chairs, rucksacks, toddlers pulling at restraint reins. Above it all an aggrieved little voice determined to tell us hers was, "a butterfly net and not, a fishing net." All the voices sounded raw in the heat of the blistering sun. Mum, Dad and I stood in silence beside our cases; there just wasn't enough air to breath and talk. Mother held a newspaper up to shade her head.

Hopes rose at the sound of an engine followed by the sight of a single deck bus lumbering into the station yard.

"Cerumbs!" Dad exclaimed, amid happy yelps and catcalls, "this one was an old banger when I was a lad." But to our dismay the bus rumbled on past our queue; followed by our groans, it stopped further along beside a group of ladies who were standing quietly with their shopping baskets. A figure unfolded his self clattering down the bus steps on feet twice as long as his body; for a moment he reminded me of the clown with long feet I had seen at Bertram Mills' circus in Preston Park, earlier in the year.

"Afternoon ladies," we heard the conductor say as he arrived beside his passengers. Helping each to board his bus he greeted every one by name as he settled all six into their seats by the door.

Our group of hopeful passengers stood dejected, mesmerised by this show of gentile behaviour, when, much to our surprise, the conductor stepped back out onto the road and turned to us giving an amused little salute saying, "Over to the Island is it? On you get then."

After another rush of bodies that almost bowled my mother over she was kindly ushered, with her precious bag of eggs held carefully out in front of her, into the next vacant seat behind the locals, while the rear of the elderly Charabanc filled; as if by a group of excited Sardines, now bosom buddies, laughing and tumbling over each other in the back seats like naughty school kids.

Looking over his shoulder in his half glass partitioned cubicle, the driver, shouted through a large orange walrus moustache. "We all ready then?" The Conductor winked at his lady passengers and called out,

"Hold tight ding-ding." raising a cheer and a roar of,

"Sunshine Holiday Camp here we come." chorused the folks in the back seats.

Sandy grit scrunched under the tyres as the Driver slowly eased his heavily laden vehicle to roll forward then a deep swirling whine came from the engine as he gently engaged second gear and we were away. Chatter in the back seats sank to a satisfied burble. Less than five minutes later the bus came to a halt and the Conductor called,

"Right you are folks everybody off, bring your bags with you." The ladies with their shopping bags were already off the bus and walking away while the rest of us were still expressing our disappointment.

"Lummie darn bus broke down already has it?" a man commented.

"Can't we wait on board, devil of a caper getting kids 'n' bags out all over again?" a mother asked,

"No, sorry madam, it's everyone off. Ol' bridge can't take the weight of a full bus." the bus Conductor explained. We could see the group of ladies had almost reached the far end of the bridge by the time the Conductor had gathered all his passengers down beside the bus, saying, "You're OK Jim, off yer blow." The Driver slowly edged the bus onto the wooden bridge, its planks giving a collection of groaning creaks as the tyres rolled forward at walking pace across its length. Not until it reached the other side did the conductor turn to us,

"Now, ladies gentlemen and sprogs," he announced, then pointing to my Father, "follow this gentleman with yer bags 'n' keep spread out an' I'll be across last." The bridge certainly did feel rickety as we walked above the water and smelly mud.

"Tide's out." Dad informed us.

We were relieved to reach the other side quickly finding our seats once again behind the smiling locals. Hot sweaty and irritable adults resettled bags and push chairs; glad to sit down, and rounded off by a small voice asking,

"Are we abroad now Dad?" A collective sigh of gentle amusement rippled through the company, as the bus trundled on its way.

Just past midday with the sun high in a clear sapphire blue sky, we were glad the sandy lane was fringed with trees dappling the road with plenty of shade.

"What's it he sir?" the Conductor asked my Father.

"Two and a half to Eastoak corner please." Dad replied.

"All the way, two five pennies and tuppence-happeny, two pinks 'n' a green." he even said, 'ding' as he clipped our tickets. Moving on, he was already chuckling as he said,

"I bet I don't know where you're for."

"Sunshine Holiday Camp." the crowd roared back. Confronting the first family he asked, "How many Mrs?" to her two and two halves he snapped out the tickets saying, "Mum, Dad and two God forbids it is."

And so the bus bounced its way on until it slowed down and the Conductor said, "Just a mo folks." before trotting away to the front, where he picked up one of his lady passenger's shopping basket and handed her down from the bus. We had stopped beside a small wicket gate in a neatly clipped hedge, where a tiny wooden bungalow stood at the end of a long Lavender edged path. Our Conductor opened the gate and ushered his passenger through, still carrying her basket, then he took her elbow and walked her all the way up the path. We could see they were deep in conversation.

At the door he handed her the basket gave a tiny little bow and walked back to the bus where both the Conductor the Driver and the five remaining ladies waved calling, "Goodbyeee." We non locals were mesmerised,

"I didn't notice she was crippled." a wag from the back remarked amongst a small collection of stifled giggles.

A little way further on a second lady stood up with her basket on her arm. The bus slowed, a groan came from behind covered by,

"Oh look what a lovely cottage." and so it was; the typical Roses round the door and Clematis climbing up over the roof. When the Conductor jumped down to help his passenger we all held our breath expecting the same performance. Instead a another lady followed and both waved their goodbyes, one crossing over to yet another small building barely visible behind the hedge on the other side of the road. The bus moved on but there were three more locals to go and now as we travelled further south the trees thinned, we were on the open road. Even though the door was open, the atmosphere was sleepy; the bus felt airless. Suddenly the Conductor told the Driver to,

"Stop," causing the tyres to squelch and squeal on the hot tarmac, in the process jerking us all awake, "looky there, Mrs Bundy's milk's still out on the step."

"Better get that in the shade for her then." suggested the Driver. The Conductor bounded, with long loping strides, up the path towards a tiny cardboard bungalow.

"Surprised the ol' Milky didn't stand the tile up to shade the bottle." said the Conductor as he skipped back on board. "He's new."

"Who's new?" asked the Conductor.

"The Milkman, 'es an ex Naval chappie, he's giving our regular man the Bank holiday off. Ah there's Mrs B over the field. Bin to take her Goats down to the water I expect."

Oh dear, were they going to stop forever jawing over the why's and wherefores of Mrs B's milk delivery. The bus trundled on, nothing passed going in the opposite direction and no more houses came into view. I expect Dad thought a change of subject would liven up our spirits, so he started to ask Mum what the screeching was all about in her compartment, when the train pulled in to Emsworth; but before she had a chance to answer, the bus slowed to a stop. A muffled sigh of, 'no not again,' erupted from the seats behind us. There weren't houses in sight but then the last three ladies, thankfully, all alighted from the bus together. As our two crew members waved them off we watched the women disappeared through the hedge coming back into sight a few moments later walking across a field.

"Soon be us next." a reassuring voice calmed the squirming children when one family moved into the vacated seats, the mother sighing, "Cor it's cooler 'ere by the door."

"Go on," Dad urged Mum, "what was all the fuss back at Emsworth then?"

"You remember that woman that trod on my feet; the one dressed up in all those frills with a big flowery sun hat?" Dad and I nodded. It really was too hot to speak, so Mum's voice was not much more than a whisper as she told us that the woman had gone to sit over by the window, facing the full force of the sun, and refused to have the window in the door right down because the black smuts flying in from the engine, would get all over her clothes. "The atmosphere in the carriage was very stuffy and a kind of sweet acid smell seemed to be filling the air. Most of the other passengers were dosing except the young man sitting opposite the big lady in the frilly dress. I could see he wasn't asleep because he had a huge grin on his face and staring straight at her, gradually lowering his newspaper to peer over the top. Well, I had to swivel myself round a bit to look along the seat to see what was tickling him so much. The frilly lady seemed to be asleep but it was something above her head that caught my eye. It took me a few moments before I realised a gooey looking liquid was dripping into the flowers on her sun hat, from a basket on the luggage rack above her head. It must have been happening for sometime because the hat was beginning to droop heavily over her face. I looked back to the chap opposite, thinking he might be about to warn her, but he had shrunk down lower behind his paper. It was painful to watch. I must say I was just as bad, I was riveted when; whoops, a drop of the liquid spilled from the edge of a petal and slithered gently down into her cleavage I thought the man opposite was going to bust, he began shaking so much; but no, he controlled it and another drip followed and the vision got worse as the dozing woman smiled and raised her fingertips to her ample bust and mumbled sleepily, 'No stop it silly.' I heard it quite clearly. Then the thought came to me that it could be brown sauce leaking from the bag above. Suddenly the train gave a small lurch causing the woman's head to bob forward the weight of the liquid spilled heavily onto her chest and down her into her cleavage. She jumped violently screeching her head off, at same time a voice on the station platform shouted, 'Emsworth.'

All the noise shook the dosing passengers awake, someone said, 'Who screamed.' And I noticed a small explosion came from the man behind the newspaper.

Hardly before the train came to a stop the woman, still screeching, heaved herself out onto the platform flapping at the brown mess on her chest. Oh dear you should have seen the horror on the faces of passengers walking passed her from the other carriages as she pushed her way across the platform and started banging her sun hat against the wall. You could see they had no idea where the brown mess came from.

Then, the lady next to me stood up and reached to get her basket off the luggage rack, and gave out her own shriek,

'Oh me sauce bottles' busted, Aw me ol' man 'el kill me, 'e loves 'is HP sauce.' That's when I knew I was right."

All the way through her story Dad and I leaned towards Mum, stifling our giggles, in anticipation of the outcome. As Mum finished she couldn't stop herself joining in, but, "Oh no Artie, we shouldn't laugh. It got worse, the poor woman had such a red hot face an' she was still out on the platform slapping her chest with a hanky when we heard the whistle go an' the train started moving again. Last I saw she was running along the platform shouting awful words." And that made Mum and Dad roll up all over again. When they calmed down Mum said, "The only other person left in the carriage was the man in the other corner and he had his paper clenched against his face. He must have felt I was looking at him, because he peered round the edge of his paper at me and we both burst out laughing together. Oh dear poor woman, I feel guilty for not warning her."

Although Mum had spoken quietly it was obvious the passengers near us had been listening because they exploded in a cloud of mirth.

"When we gonna get there?" a sad little voice behind us pleaded; touchy words parleyed and a small boy received a cuff round the ear. To that little boy the journey must have felt interminable.

"Nobody here for Sunshine Holidee Camp is there? Drive on Bill!" the back of the bus jolted on its tyres; the cheering crowd fairly flung itself out onto the sandy lane. Push chairs restored to their rightful shapes were piled with bags, a Dad turned away carrying a sleepy toddler and a child scrambled back onto the bus to retrieve a doll, before the whole group marched off along the lane where a finger post pointed out, 'To the Holiday Camp.'

"Not much further folks," We hadn't gone far when the Driver turned to us, "Where you headed for?" Dad pulled a piece of paper out of the breast pocket of his sports jacket and read out, "Eastoak Caravan Park."

"Ah we might as well drop you off here then, this here's the lane what leads right there. Bit of a long walk but keep going you can't miss it."

"Good luck have a nice time." the Conductor and the Driver chorused, "See yer next Saturday mornin,' shall we?" the conductor asked, "have a good time then, cheerio." We stood for a few moments taking a breather.

"Come on," said Dad, the track was rough but thankfully shaded by high overgrown hedges on each side. If we had a long walk at least here we were cooler.

I think the conductor had been trying to give us a pleasant surprise because it was only a few steps before we came to a five bar gate, beyond that we could see a variety of old vehicles, bathed in bright sunlight. Referring to his piece of paper Dad read out, "Turn right and straight on to the corner plot."

Either side of the wide gritted path old railway carriages and single deck buses stood in their own fenced areas. Some had neatly laid out garden borders, others mown lawns with children's toys strewn around; there were little steps up to front doors and flower covered porches and even a double-decker bus, decorated with colourful hanging baskets at each corner still displaying, 'Portsmouth Dockyard,' on its destination board. Mum said,

"What a picture." By now it was after two o clock and apart from a couple of elderly gentlemen with knotted hankies on their heads snoozing in deckchairs, there didn't appear to be any other human life in sight. There was something else. A strange smell in the air seemed to be getting stronger as we got further along the field.

Standing deep in the tall grass our holiday destination looked very forlorn. A long shed like structure, made of faded cream and brown wood boarding with large windows, seemed to be perched on four perished rubber tyres. It was difficult to tell if it had once been an old bus or a railway carriage. Woodland closely edged two sides; the other two sides of the plot sported a chain link fence, festooned with white belled convolvulus flowers.

"Come on we'll soon find out Dad said, climbing the squeaky wooden steps as he pulled a big old key, from his inside pocket. "Doors stuck!" I had visions of sleeping outside in the foot high grass, but a good shove with Dad's shoulder took him skidding inside and us reeling back away from a blast of hot stuffy air. "Ernie said nobody had been here for a few weeks."

"You can tell that by the long grass." Mum said, stating the obvious..

"Yes, well I told Ernie I'd run the mower over that for him." Mum and I followed Dad through the first two compartments; each divided by sliding doors, a bed either side, covered by two grey army blankets and a pillow under a large window. Mum eased the curtains open flooding the space with light and more heat. At the far end a wooden shed made a small dining area with a table and benches fitted to the walls; in one corner a set of shallow shelves above a cupboard served as a dinky sized dresser to hold crockery: four of everything. Dad unlatched the windows on each side of a glass panelled door above another flight of wooden steps down into the long grass.

"Phew nice to get out of that heat, but oh dear that smell's awful whatever do you think it is Artie?"

"That must be the old creek behind the trees here. Ernie says it niffs a bit in the hot weather."

"Did ERNIE say where the kitchen is?" Mum said tartly.

"Yeah, there's a shed on the side of the plot against the trees look." And of course when Dad finally found the key under a flower pot and unlocked the door, it was like an oven inside there too. The kitchen boasted a small table with a Baby Belling oven and hot plate; on another table a kettle and saucepan sat in a chipped enamel washing-up bowl; underneath that stood a large metal bucket and a tall jug.

To me everything was magic, just like a camp in the woods; the 'Secret Seven and Famous Five all rolled into one.

"Where's the lavatory?" Mum wanted to know.

"Ah that must have been in that big shed beside the entrance gate." Mum groaned it was a long walk if you were caught short.

After a brief investigation to find the washing facilities we walked across the lane to the row of shops on the seafront; all closed as it was Saturday afternoon.

Opposite the shops the narrow seafront road gave way to a rough edge of tufty grass and a wide shallow sandy beach. I could not help but gasp at the sight, so different from Brighton's horrible great pebbles sloping down into the water. Here on Hayling Island's southern shore, pale creamy sand stretched, without a break in both directions, as far as you could see away into the heat haze.

In the twilight on our first evening, the heat of the day still rose off the soft sand where we strolled along the tide line. Across the sea, a necklace of tiny lights glittered along the edge of a dark mound against the deep blue velvet sky.

The air smelled full of a flowery perfume; Dad said it was probably wafting over to us from all the gardens on the Isle of Wight.

I thought this must be the most beautiful peaceful place in the whole world.

It didn't matter that the bed was hard and the blanket was rough; nor even that the old timber framed carriage began to grumble and squeak, as it eased itself into the freshening night air. I slept through a thunder storm and torrential rain into a glistening clear new day.

I woke the next morning with a strange feeling I was alone. All I could hear was a soft swishing sound. Lifting the edge of the curtain I saw trees swaying in the breeze. It didn't take me a minute to jump out of bed and run out into the grass in my bare feet. Here there were no stairs, no walls, no coal shed and dustbin to pass before I could reach the little grass patch we called, the garden, at the back of our house in Coventry street; and nobody to tell me to put something on my feet, just pure freedom. I skipped through the wet grass my pyjama trousers getting soaked, it didn't matter, the wide open space the warm morning air and the quiet of a summer Sunday morning. Bliss, I kicked up the long strands of grass cuttings Dad had made the evening before. I picked them up in bundles and threw them in the air, flung it around to spread it in whirls over my head. One day I would have a big garden with lots of space to dance around, that's what I'd have. Oh yes, and a tree.

"Wheee-whirl. Ah." There was my father standing by the gate carrying a bucket, a wide smile on his face. Mum popped out of the kitchen shed a fish slice and a tea-towel in her hand and an enquiring look on her face. Catching sight of Dad's smile she withdrew back to her cooking.

"Lucky I decided to give the grass a cut last evening there must have been a heavy downpour in the night." He said. Obviously he slept well too. Clang, went the bucket as Dad returned it to its place down behind the shed; another of Ernie's neat conveniences we had discovered before we went to bed.

Bacon, eggs, bread butter marmalade and tea round the table in the caravan's dolls house sized kitchen, with the glass door open allowing the outside in, everything smelled so wonderfully fresh and clean. Washed, dressed, breakfasted, washing up done, potatoes, Mum called tiny chats, scraped and left in a bowl of water ready to cook for dinner, the three of us set off for the seafront shops to buy the Sunday newspapers. *News of the World* for Dad, a *Reveille* for Mum and *School Friend* for me, ½oz of Juggler tobacco for Dad, 5 Weights cigarettes for Mum and 2ozs of sherbet lemons from my ration book points for me. Then it was across the road to see the sea and the beach again. At home in Brighton I had never bothered about the beach, to me it was a dirty place that hurt your feet if you didn't wear shoes; and when you did wear shoes little stones always found their way in, and besides that you had to be watchful not to step in the great lumps of tar that frequently washed up on the pebbles. No this was somewhere quite different. Here was heaven, soft sand under your feet. The view that Sunday morning took my breath away all over again.

The Isle of Wight lit bright in the rising sun was like a moving picture in miniature. I could pick out people walking along the seafront and cars gliding back and forth; rows of small houses their windows glinting like smiling eyes. Green hills rose up behind the buildings so clear that tiny white pathways across their sides looked just like pencil lines. Sharp white pointed sails smoothed over the sea in all directions. Life, that day looked full of colour and people, with happy faces enjoying themselves. It set the pattern of our week.

Before breakfast each morning Dad and I walked down to the newsagent's shop on the seafront, bought his newspaper then skipped, or I did, across the sand strewn road to see the view of the Island to find it was different every day. One day we could only see a deep dark hazy mauve lump on the horizon. Another morning, while we stood in warm sunshine, blocks of grey clouds moving visibly quite fast over the Island opposite, sending down dark curtains of rain onto the land chased away by beams of bright clear sunshine. I could hardly tear myself away from this wonderful moving weather picture, but usually my father wanted to go back to the caravan and read his paper.

My explorations into the nether regions all started rather tentatively. There were no fences, nothing to stop me wandering in among the strange gnarled old trees edging our corner of the caravan field. When we arrived in the overblown heat on Saturday afternoon the smell that filled the air nearly sent my mother home, but after the first night of rain we woke to, well, nothing. For a short spell in the beautiful morning fresh air, we didn't even notice there was no horrible smell. A narrow wrinkly path wound its way along the margin of the field behind the trees, following a wide shining expanse of water, a narrow strip of blue sky mirrored down its centre, on either bank the underside of branches were reflected in the water. I sat down on the weedy edge to watch. Almost no sound, quiet and cool, nothing moving, not even a breeze. Being an only child I was used to watching alone undisturbed.

"What you lookin' for?" whispered a boy's voice from nearby on the bank. Although the voice had surprised me I didn't look round,

"Anything." I answered.

"Any what?" he asked.

"Whatever lives here." I told him.

"Girls are not usually funny." I didn't bother to answer. A tiny vole ran up the bank opposite; at the same moment I could hear my Gran's soft voice saying, 'Water Vole,' in my memory's ear.

"See that?" the boy whispered excitedly. He all but fell down into the water in his haste to get across the water in pursuit. I wished he had fallen in. Why couldn't he keep still and just watch, instead his next step went ankle deep in sucking black mud revealing where the nasty smell from Saturday lay in wait. "Urgh, my Mum'll kill me!" I grabbed his arm before he toppled and got both his plimsoled feet black. He slunk off dejectedly back along the path to the caravan field, I didn't expect to see him again.

My parents were people of routine. Every morning we fetched the newspapers and walked across onto the wide sandy beach to look at the view. On the Monday morning Dad had forgotten it was bank holiday so there were no newspapers.

"Come on," he said, "let's explore." Together we walked east away from the caravan field, as far as the path went before it petered out into a meandering reed bed to the sea. Across the water we had a long view to Chichester harbour, full of bobbing little sails. Mum never came on our explorations she didn't like walking on uneven ground, so we didn't stay long, "Better get back to Mum we'll go and have a lunch time drink."

Ernie had given Dad directions to a pub with a children's room, so on Saturday evening we had walked along the dunes towards Eastoak point and discovered the Meeth Hotel. We found a spacious room with huge windows giving a view over the water to Chichester. In the centre of the room stood a half size Bar Billiard table surrounded by groups of family tables with comfortable chairs. On shelves beside the bar was a selection of games like Draughts, Dominos and Ludo to take to the tables. A dart board hung on the wall, well out of the way over to one side. This family

room was the first time I had not had to stand outside a pub or
be allowed in a side passageway if it was bad weather. Dad and I
played Bar Billiards. We liked it so much Dad booked us a session
for every lunch time for the rest of the week and some evenings
too. Mum sat at a different table each day, thoroughly enjoying
talking and having a laugh with other families and sometimes
leading a sing song just before closing time. There were no snacks
at the bar except crisps; the hotel only served food to its residents,
so Mum cooked us a midday meal that we ate back at the caravan,
about 2o/c each day. There were no places to eat out and anyway
my parents couldn't afford that kind of life style.

In the evenings we played a round of miniature Golf on a small
green on the seafront before walking along the grassy sand dunes
to the hotel games room. At closing time we picked our way to the
caravan field along the well trod path to a sand strewn lane, where
it was safer under foot in the twilight of the summer night.

On Wednesday something different happened. Our next door
neighbour from Coventry Street came to visit us for the day. As
a retired Railway man he could travel by train for free. Uncle Bert
had spent all his working life on the Railways, travelling all over
England. On the bookshelves in his front room he had a great
collection of books from everywhere he had been in the British
Isles. He was very proud of this country and looking at the pictures
in his books filled many a winter evening. He left some of his
books to me and I still have them. The black and white photos and
engravings show a quiet peaceful car free country.

The single line railway track followed the west side of Hayling
Island, ending at a small station halfway down the island far away
from Eastoak. So we walked along the seaside then up inland
along a leafy country lane to meet his train. At exactly 12 noon an
old puffing Billy engine drew along-side the platform opposite the
ticket office waiting room. The few passengers that left the cream
and brown carriages gave their tickets to the collector at the gate,
who greeted each by name and they called him Joe. No sign of

Uncle Bert though. Two men, who appeared to be old friends by the way they were sharing their conversation, descended from the far end of the train and began walking along the platform towards us. One wearing a uniform and a cap with a badge, the other man, a head taller, wore a neat Sunday suit with a gold watch chain across the front of his waistcoat, a very smart Trilby hat set at a slightly jaunty angle, and highly polished shoes. Suddenly I realised the taller man was my Uncle Bert, who I had only ever seen in a flat cap with his sleeves rolled up and wearing an apron wrapped round his portly middle – a sacking apron for cleaning jobs and white cotton for cooking. As I was holding the brownie box camera I immediately, without asking permission, it was my mother's camera, raised it to waist height looked down into the little window and pressed the shutter. Seeing me he stopped politely for a second then walked on towards the engine where the Fireman stood on the platform and the engine driver up on the footplate.

"Thank you Mr Jones said Uncle Bert holding up his hand; the engine driver leaned down and took the offered hand saying,

"A privilege to have you on board Mr Pearless, like old times, look forward to taking you home." When Uncle Bert turned to the fireman the man whipped off his greasy cotton cap and wiped his hand down his overalls before taking the hand held out to him and I feel sure he almost bowed. By then the ticket collector had donned a bowler hat and turned into the station master standing to attention beside his ticket office. All smiles the two men shook hands.

"How's retirement Albert, wish you were back on the roads eh?"

"No" replied Uncle Bert, "I'm enjoying my wine making and just pleasing myself Jack. How are the wife and family?"

"All's well, I'll tell the wife I've seen you. Have a grand visit."

Dad said that Uncle Bert was Railway royalty. He'd been one of the top men in his day. During the war years he was a mainstay organising and keeping the tracks open. As a ganger he and the engine drivers were kings of the roads, top men on the railway system.

This new man of such consequence seemed to me rather out of place eating dinner in our tiny caravan kitchen but by the time we had finished the meal he and my parents had laughed a lot. Once again he was the jolly old Uncle Bert I knew so well.

Walking back to the station in the early evening we stood at the side of the sandy seafront road while uncle Bert gazed across the water saying what a lovely sight it was to see the dear old Isle of Wight again, then in a quiet, wistful voice, he told my parents,

"Mrs Peerless and I spent our honeymoon there back in 1890, that's when the old Queen was on throne in those days."

It was hand-shakes all round on the station platform, even the station master's wife had come across to the station saying she just couldn't miss saying hallo to dear Albert. After that the Railway ritual played the same scene again, only this time in reverse. Shaking hands with the driver the fireman the station master, everybody was very polite. Turning to us he said, "Thanks for a grand day."

"See you on Saturday." Mum said and Dad called out his usual salutation,

"Bye Squire." We waved, watching the engine chuff gently away along the flat track for quite a long time, before turning to walk south to the seaside. Dad said, "We've known Bert and Mrs Peerless for twenty years through good times and war and yet it's the first time we've heard anything about their life together before 1936." No more was spoken on the long walk on the sands to the Meeth hotel where my parents would have a drink and we hoped we could book a game on the bar billiard table.

One week goes so quickly and Thursday morning was next to our last day. With the sound of water trickling over fallen branches accompanied by the blick-blick warnings of many tiny birds, I crouched deep beside the tangled reeds on the banks of the creek. The mud here felt all plastic and just right for making little pots, my mind was far away as I put the finishing touches to a deep bowl in the palm of my hand. Stretching out to pull on a long strand of flat grass a Blackbird shattered the silence with its sharp alarm call. It crossed my mind that my small movement wouldn't have frightened that bird when a soft conspiratorial voice asked, "Is it still there, the mouse?"

"No." I knew who it was, "There's a water rat just inside that hole there. Look." The boy quietly inched his way along the bank hunkering down beside me.

"Where were you yesterday? I came down to see if that vole was over there." Finally succeeding in gathering the grass I needed I began to wind a strand round my bowl patting it into the soft clay surface.

"We had a visitor."

"Mum said your parents weren't in the bar lunch time. My Mum likes talking to your mother." I know Mum enjoyed meeting and talking to people at the hotel bar but I had never seen the boy there.

"I like playing the bar billiards with my Dad."

"My parents said I can't go in with them because I'm only nine, but I'll be ten soon." He said full of excitement.

"I'll be ten in January."

"How did you get in the bar then?"

"It's a children's room." He didn't speak for a while then he said,

"My parents make me stay in the caravan when they go to the pub in the evenings." with growing understanding, he explained, "I just mess around on the sea shore at lunch times." He whined. I began to feel sorry for him,

"Haven't you got any brothers and sisters?" I asked.

"Nope, well they're grown up and don't come on holiday with us."

"Dad's booked a session on the billiards table for us tonight why don't you come, children can come in?"

As soon as we arrived at the children's room that evening, Mum went to sit at a table with eight empty chairs, "There'll be lots of people in soon." She said as Dad brought her a gin and orange across from the bar. I had told my parents about the boy and they said what a shame to leave him all on his own when it was his holiday too. Later a lady and gentleman, a bit older than my parents, joined Mum at the table. I saw the boy leaning on the balustrade outside on the terrace. When I waved to him I was surprised to see him immediately slunk back out of sight.

"Is that your son?" My Mum asked the lady sitting beside her.

"Where?" her reply shot back.

"Over there by the door. Good looking little chap isn't he?" Mum said.

"I'll give him good lookin' if his father sees 'im he'll be for it."

"Dad says he can come and join our game." I thought it might help.

"Oh I hadn't realised this is your girl." Her voice seemed to soften.

"Please." I pleaded.

"Young monkey," The boy's mother said, "he should be in bed."

I skipped speedily across to the boy, before his Mum could change her mind. He shrunk back into the shadows again so I took hold of his hand and pulling him through the door telling him,

"Your Mum says it's alright for you to play with us." He followed, although somewhat reluctantly, and stood beside my Dad at the billiard table. I noticed how he stayed close to my father keeping him between the direct sight of where his Mum, and now his Dad sat at the table.

"Come on old chap," my Father said, "let's get you a cue. Have you played before?" It wasn't very long before we were all engrossed in our game and the boy was laughing along with me and Dad when we missed a mark. While we were tidying the balls away, sad that our time was up, Dad went to the bar and bought us each an orange squash to take to the table. The boy's father didn't look very pleased as he thanked my Dad for including, 'The boy,' as he called him.

Although I was enjoying having my long hair brushed out in the garden each morning it was our last morning so I was impatient to look at the clay pots I had left baking in the sun outside the kitchen shed the previous day. But for the moment I had to stand still while Mum gave my hair its usual hundred brushes; my hair was so thick it was lovely having it brushed, out in the warm air, allowing the breeze
to carry the loose strands flying up into the trees. When the brushing was finished and two pigtails plaited, I was free to find my pots; the clay had shrunk away from the grass I had woven round the outside of the bowl shapes, leaving separate little baskets and pots, all ready to take home. I planned to put them in our oven when Mum cooked the Sunday dinner.

I wandered along the pathway beside the creek to see if the water vole would show itself again and found the boy was sitting quietly in my watching spot. Time seemed to stand still in the morning sun. He was just pointing out a tiny hole in the opposite bank, when my father's voice called from back along the path, "Where are you, we're getting ready to go and have a drink." I never saw the boy again and never knew his name.

Frying times at the Fish and Chip shop on the seafront were Saturday lunchtime and Friday evening so we had missed the opening times when we arrived on our first weekend. On our last evening in the caravan we had fish and chips all ready to eat which was a relief for Mum from cooking. We bought two 1/6 Cod and two thruppeny portions of chips for Mum and Dad and a ninepenny piece of Cod with two-pennorth of chips for me. All swathed around with layers of newspaper to keep it warm as we walked back to the caravan to eat with my favourite Dinky Chop sauce and lovely crusty new bread. Finding the fresh baker's bread was a bit of luck. It came about because Mum had stayed at the

186

caravan to clear up and pack a few things on Friday morning instead of walking down to the seafront with Dad and me. As she was hanging out the washing a yodelling by the gate attracted her attention,

"Any bread today Mrs?" a man called from a horse drawn bread van, "I call round the site on Fridays would you like some bread today?" Yes it would be a lovely teatime treat, and would leave the whole sliced loaf, she had ordered from the seafront shop, to make corned beef sandwiches for our journey home in the train the next day. The shop on the beach parade also sold sterilised milk; my only reason to be looking forward to getting home again was having fresh milk. Although Mum had to boil and cool our milk every day in the summer months, we were used to that. This was the first time I had tasted sterilised milk and I did not like it.

Early on Saturday morning Dad carried our cases along to the seafront parade where the bus started its first run of the day. The driver and conductor greeted us like old friends asking us how we had enjoyed our week; telling Mum what a lovely tan she had while ushering her to the seats one row back from the front. The driver helped Dad up with the cases jokingly remarking how much lighter they were now we had eaten all the rations we had brought with us. For five minutes we were the sole passengers before the first stop at the end of the lane leading to the Sunshine Holiday camp. Although there was nobody waiting the driver stopped the bus beside the little rusty old bus stop sign buried in the hedge.

"Don't worry folks." The conductor said, "They're always late from the Holiday camp."

"You'll hear them before you see them." Chortled the driver; and so we did. Soon there they were hollering, 'Stop, wait.' as they came into view running; yelping, tripping over the pushchairs, butterfly nets, flags and balloons. All the paraphernalia of fun; the same faces from last Saturday arrived scrambling up the steps, one saying to us,

"Hallo, haven't seen you about, where did you get to all week?"
not waiting for an answer amid their joshing laughter, ouches,
stop-
its and sighs of relief while they settled into their seats at the rear
of
the bus.

At the next stop three ladies climbed onto the bus greeting
us all with cheerful recognition. By the time we reached the old
wooden bridge the locals with their empty shopping baskets had
all taken their usual seats and the bus was full of a friendly buzz.

"Come on kids up n'at it." called a voice from the back. The
driver
and conductor laughed, no bother this time trying to explain the
procedure, their passengers mustered in a sombre group watching
as the bus moved gently onto the bridge trundling forward at
walking
pace over the old planking. We let the locals walk ahead while we
and
our fellow holiday makers paused briefly to tell each other about
our
holiday. We hadn't seen or even heard any of the noisy shenanigans
they described because they had not put their noses outside the
holiday camp gates, so we told them a little about Hayling Island's
beautiful beaches, which they, so they told us, had not seen.
However the consensus was we had all enjoyed our week away
from the daily grind.

This was a cooler Saturday in many ways. For a start the
temperature was lower than the previous weekend, when
everybody seemed to be at a bank holiday fever pitch; raring to get
away and have a good time. Back then there were more people,
more baggage blocking the train corridors, frayed tempers followed
by plenty of joking and nervous laughter.

Now, here we were, the three of us on the train seated in a
compartment, going home in a much more subdued atmosphere,

waiting quietly opposite just two other passengers. A lady and gentleman; he was wearing a dog collar, both appeared to be deeply engrossed in reading their respective books, when,

"Come on darlin', there's two seats in 'ere." The carriage door opened with a crash back on its hinges, and in climbed the stout lady; she wasn't wearing a sun hat but this time her frilly dress was covered in huge pink cabbage roses. She was followed by a fresh faced young sailor who, seeing the lady sitting opposite whipped his little round white cap off and nodded politely in hers and my Mum's direction before taking his seat.

All went quiet as our fellow passengers took in the lady and her sailor boy. Recognising my Mum, the frilly lady squawked out a laugh, saying,

"'ope nobody's got a bottle of brown sauce up on that luggage rack!" Of course, my parents joined in with her laughter, bringing glares from the couple opposite. Noting this reaction the stout lady put her arm round the sailor's shoulder and said, in what sounded a very provocative voice,

"Lovely, isn't he?" the man looked shocked, whilst his companion made a face of pure contempt. The pair got off the train at the next stop. As soon as the door closed behind them the lady turned to us and said, "Meet my youngest, 'es just got his first leave, 'es doing 'is National Service you know. Have a good holiday did you dears? Aw! And how's yer feet love."

Author's note

*I hope you have enjoyed this first chapter about 1950s life.
The sun always seemed to shine. People were light hearted;
not surprising after the 1940s.*

*I noticed, when I described the station ticket collector shouted,
"Order." The crowd immediately responded for, of course the
majority of people had been so used to taking orders in the Forces.
But it was all good hearted.*

*We had to take all our food with us, for at least the weekend as
there were no shops allowed to sell food; only sweets cigarettes
and newspapers on a Sunday morning.*

*On tiny sparsely inhabited Hayling Island the Fish and Chip shop
only opened on Friday evening and Saturday lunch time.
Rather like the Fish shop at the end of our street.*

*There were no plastic bottles, only heavy glass bottles to carry milk
in and no polythene bags to keep food fresh.*

*Looking back, I see Hayling Island would have been a perfect
paradise for honeymooners.*

Acknowledgements

Thank you, Galia, for encouraging me to write my grandmother's stories.

My love and thanks to Paul who has supported me in everything I have done in the 54 years we have been together.

My special thanks to Ollie Wardle who typed my original manuscript and helped me through my battles with wayward computers. Ollie you are a star.

And of course I must express thanks to all my relatives and friends who have demonstrated their enthusiasm for my writing giving much appreciated comments.

Clara's richly illuminated story makes me wish I could chart my own grandmother's life with such depth and clarity. I could not put *Single to Brighton* down. Nor can I wait to hear, in the second volume, what happened next to the intrepid Clara.

**The Eminent Historian
Professor Lisa Jardine CBE**

Dolly's story has all the narrative excitement of the roaring twenties. It is full of the sights and sounds of the period, and shot through with the emotions of the age.

**The Eminent Historian
Professor Lisa Jardine CBE**

Clara recalls the flavour and sights she experienced in her childhood on the Pevensey Levels in the 1870-80s. Then it's Lilian's turn to tell the sorrows, surprises and happiness that surrounded Clara in her last ten years.

Find out more about Lilian and her writing
www.singltobrighton.co.uk

Lilian Forshaw was born in Brighton, Sussex and studied at Brighton Art College, where she specialised in painting and Industrial pottery before spending time painting in Venice. In her final year she trained to be an art teacher, and has continued to explore new techniques and media throughout her life, most recently becoming an award winning portrait painter.

Encouraged by her daughter to, 'write down all the family stories her grandmother had told her' she made a start when she retired and surprised herself when, in less than two years she had written four books; a trilogy, covering the years 1887 to 1952 about family life in Brighton.
The fourth book is a prequel telling a tale from the wider Sussex family in the 1770s to 1874.

Lilian now lives near Battle in East Sussex.